'I don't care for company,
I don't care for yours.'

When Abigail Tarrant is [...] Sophie Farraday to join her father in India, she is shocked by the coldness of their reception. For Brett Farraday, ruthless owner of the ruby mines in Mandara, makes it quite clear that both she and his own daughter are an unwelcome intrusion.

Why does Brett have such a vengeful anger against the past? And what really happened to Sophie mother? His cold-blooded decision about their future only reinforces the enmity between them. But Abigail is torn, for she has fallen under the magical spell of Mandara. . .

Devil's Fire
Jean Evans

MILLS & BOON LIMITED
London · Sydney · Toronto

First published in Great Britain 1983
by Mills & Boon Limited, 15–16 Brook's Mews,
London W1A 1DR

ISBN 0 263 74420 5

Set in 10 on 11½ pt Linotron Times
04/1083

Photoset by Rowland Phototypesetting Ltd
Bury St Edmunds, Suffolk
Made and printed in Great Britain by
Cox & Wyman Ltd, Reading, Berks.

CHAPTER
ONE

'BEFORE you come to any decision you are entitled to know the truth, Miss Tarrant.' Lady Flixton's agitated pacing ceased as she paused to look out of the window on to the windswept lawns below. After a moment her glance turned to the young woman seated across the room. 'It isn't easy. . .'

A slight pensiveness marked Abigail's features beneath her plain bonnet as she set down her cup. 'Then I beg you not to trouble yourself with it, Ma'am. I am sure there is no need.'

'On the contrary.' A tremor shook Lady Flixton's frail hand. 'There is every need. I should be failing in my duty were I to allow you to accept without warning you of the kind of man Brett Farraday is.' The pale lips compressed for a moment. 'He killed my niece, Miss Tarrant. As surely as if he had murdered her with his own hands. That is the kind of man he is.'

'But. . . I don't understand.' Abigail felt as if she were frozen to the spot.

Lady Flixton turned, her hands clenching and unclenching. 'No, I'm sure you could not. But it is true. He stormed into my niece's life. Within a few weeks they were married, shortly afterwards he carried her off to India, and within two years she was dead.'

Abigail felt the colour drain from her face as she stared, uncomprehending. 'But what happened?'

'As to that, I fear we may never know the full truth.'

Anger hardened Lady Flixton's voice. 'But he should
never have taken her out there. I knew it was a mistake
and within weeks her letters confirmed it. Elaina hated
that country. She hated the heat, the loneliness and
above all she hated the man she had married.'

A frown disfigured Abigail's features as she reached
blindly for the support of a chair. Though not by any
standards a beauty, there was at that moment a certain
attraction in the wide mouth and the blue eyes, clouded
with confusion. Her hand fluttered to the high collar of
her gown, as if, suddenly, it restricted her breathing.
'Did she ever tell you what had caused this change in her
affections?'

Lady Flixton's hand rose. 'It was easy to see. The
simple truth was that the man she had married in such
foolish haste bore little or no resemblance to the man she
discovered once they had returned to India.'

Abigail shook her head. 'Forgive me, I find it hard to
understand. In what way did he change?'

'Elaina spoke very little about it. I know only that he
became almost a stranger to her. She was left alone a
great deal, a stranger in a strange country. Oh yes, she
had servants but there was no one to whom she could
speak, to whom she could turn as a friend, and all of
these things were important to Elaina.' Her glance
lifted. 'You were not acquainted with my niece, Miss
Tarrant. She was a social butterfly, hot-headed, wil-
ful. . . India must have been like a prison to her.'

'But surely, if they were in love. . .'

'Love.' The word rasped on Lady Flixton's lips. 'If he
had loved her he would never have condemned her to
such a life, he would have seen what it was doing to her.
But I hold myself as much to blame. She lacked a
mother's guidance. I begged my brother many times to

remarry but he chose instead to gamble and drink himself to death, leaving to me the responsibility of rearing his child. Well, I did it to the best of my ability and failed.'

'I think you blame yourself too harshly, Ma'am,' Abigail demurred. 'You have daughters of your own to consider.'

'Even so, perhaps I should have prevented the marriage. God knows, I have lived with that thought these past ten years.'

'What could you have done?'

The frail hands rose and fell impotently. 'I am ashamed to say that, like my brother, I chose the easy way. It was not as if in all other respects the match was not suitable. To the contrary, Brett Farraday was a far better catch than I might have hoped for for my niece. She had no fortune and with my own girls to provide for. . .' She crossed to the fire, an elegantly attired figure in brown silk, the long draped skirts rustling softly. 'Was I wrong?' She stared into the flames. 'The irony was that almost as soon as she returned to England, Elaina discovered that she was pregnant.'

'But then surely if her husband knew. . .'

'He wasn't told.' Lady Flixton's greying head rose sharply. 'Elaina was adamant. I argued with her but she was hysterical and I had no choice but to agree.' She sighed. 'It was an easy birth but it was almost as if she had lost the will to live, even for the child's sake. She died within a few days of the birth.'

'Oh no.' Abigail felt as if an icy hand had gripped her. 'But did the father make no attempt to claim the child?'

'I wrote to him. I swore to Elaina that I wouldn't but I felt it my duty. His reply was curt to the point of rudeness. He seemed to feel no remorse at her death,

and as far as the baby was concerned he said simply that
there was no place for her at Mandara.' She looked up,
seeming suddenly older. 'I have abided by his wishes all
these years. It wasn't difficult. Sophie is a sweet child but
already I begin to see in her the same wilfulness, the
spirit I saw in Elaina, and because of that I have come to
a decision.' She clasped her hands together. 'I have
decided to send the child to her father.'

Abigail couldn't prevent the gasp which broke from
her. 'To India? You mean you would send her to a total
stranger, to a strange country?'

'I have no choice.' The words were clipped. 'You
disapprove.' It was statement rather than question and
for a moment Abigail stared at her uncomprehendingly.

'I can hardly think my opinion is of any account.'

'But you think me harsh?'

Abigail bit her lip. 'I can only think that it will seem a
very cruel decision to a child who, through no fault of her
own, has never known her mother to be deprived suddenly of those whom she must regard as her only remaining family.'

Lady Flixton's features relaxed momentarily. 'It is not
my intent to be cruel, Miss Tarrant, but the time has
come when I must face reality. I am no longer young and
Sophie needs someone who can provide for her as I
cannot.' The grey eyes looked directly into Abigail's.
'Who better than her own father? It is time he undertook
his responsibilities towards her.'

'But he has never known her.'

'Then he must learn.' Lady Flixton turned away. 'We
must all do things in this life which we may not like.'

Abigail stood for a moment, her voice frozen in her
throat. 'And precisely what part is it that you wish me to
play, Lady Flixton?'

The grey eyes studied her shrewdly, taking in the high-necked gown, its moulded bodice emphasising a slender waist, the skirts draped to a small train.

'How old are you, Miss Tarrant? Nineteen?'

'I am twenty-two.'

Surprise flickered briefly in the woman's eyes and she inclined her head slowly. 'You are not married?'

'No.'

'There must have been offers. You are not unattractive. No beauty, it is true, but your figure is good.' She frowned. 'Black does not become you.'

Abigail felt the faint flush in her cheeks. 'No, it does not, but I am still in mourning for my father.'

'Ah yes, I recall. He died recently?'

'Some months ago. He had been ill for some time, which is mainly why I did not marry. My duty was to him.'

'You speak as if it still exists.'

Abigail's lips formed a stiff smile. 'At twenty-two, Ma'am, I have no false hopes that I shall marry now.'

'I know it is the fashion to marry young, but one is not always obliged to follow fashion slavishly,' Lady Flixton said, gently. 'However, your circumstances were made known to me by Mrs Amersham who recommended you to me, and perhaps it is as well there are no ties.'

'I am still not precisely clear as to what it is you require of me, Ma'am.'

'No.' She considered Abigail carefully for a moment. 'I wish someone of maturity and sensibility to escort Sophie out to India, to place her in the guardianship of her father and to remain with her for a few weeks or until such time as he has made whatever arrangements he deems necessary for her well-being. I am persuaded, Miss Tarrant, that you would be a suitable person to undertake such a task. Of course you would be free to return to England the moment the mission was accomplished to your entire satisfaction. You would, naturally, be well paid, and all arrangements for your passage to Bombay and back to England taken care of.'

Abigail stood unmoving, her brain trying to assimilate the enormity of the proposition. To go all the way to India, to be obliged to meet the very man against whom she already felt a burning resentment? Doubt must have reflected on her pale face for Lady Flixton said. 'I assure you, I have no wish to condemn Sophie to a life of poverty. Her father is a wealthy man and can well provide for her, indeed, to a far better degree than I could ever hope to do.' She hesitated, frowning for a moment, then crossed to a small bureau from which she took a box. 'This was his gift to my niece on their wedding day.' Opening the box she took something out and held it on the palm of her hand, staring at it for a moment. She held the object out to Abigail. 'Oh no, Miss Tarrant, no matter in what other respect he failed Elaina he always lavished his wealth upon her. It was a pity he had no heart to give with it.'

Abigail took the thing with trembling hands, gasping involuntarily as she stared at the stone glittering in the palm of her hand. For a moment she almost dropped it as the ruby seemed to burn her skin with its brilliance. 'It's beautiful,' she breathed. 'Like fire. I've never seen anything like it.'

'Devil's fire, Miss Tarrant, that was what my niece called it. I haven't taken it from that box since the day she died. I couldn't bear to look at it. So beautiful and yet so cold, almost like blood caught in ice.'

Abigail's hand still trembled but the woman made no move to take the stone.

'Do you doubt that Sophie will do better with her father, Miss Tarrant?'

'Can you be sure you are not condemning her to the same fate as her mother? What if he will not accept her or if she cannot accept him? He is, after all a total stranger.'

The lined face hardened. 'She is his blood. Brett Farraday took my niece from me, I am giving him his daughter. Can that be injustice?'

Abigail felt the ruby bite into the palm of her hand as she clenched her fist. 'And if I cannot do as you ask?'

Lady Flixton's hand rose. 'It is of little consequence. I shall find another.' She looked directly at Abigail. 'You see, Miss Tarrant, my mind is quite made up. But I hope you will consider carefully and decide to accept. You have met Sophie. She liked you.'

'Yes. I liked her too.' Her voice seemed to be stuck in her throat as she remembered the brief meeting with the dark-eyed little girl. Slowly she unclenched her hand and held out the ring but Lady Flixton made no move to take it.

'It is Sophie's now. Perhaps some day she will care to wear it. Keep it for her, if, that is, you wish to do as I ask.'

Suddenly Abigail hated the jewel as much as she hated the giver. What kind of man was he, she wondered, who would allow his young bride to die of loneliness and a broken heart? To what kind of future was Sophie being condemned?

'Very well,' she heard herself say. 'I will do as you ask. I will take her to her father.'

Lady Flixton's expression didn't change, though she nodded. 'I am glad. Arrangements will be made so that you may leave as soon as possible and I shall write to inform them of your intended arrival at Mandara.'

Mandara. Mandara. The name pounded in her brain like a devil that refused to be driven out. A face seemed to hover above her own, the eyes dark, the mouth cruel yet sensuous. Abigail moved her head restlessly against the pillow but he came closer and closer.

She woke with a start, exhausted and trembling, to look around her. It had been a dream, yet so vivid that even now she couldn't banish the feeling that someone had actually stood over her, touched her.

She lay back trying to gather her wits. Her lips were parched. She pressed a hand to her throat and neck. The skin was damp with sweat even though she had stripped off her gown to lie down wearing only her long petticoat. There was no relief from the heat, it was constant and suffocating.

Her hair, free of its pins, fell thickly in waves about her shoulders as she sat up, slowly, trying to fight off the remaining cobwebs of what felt like a drugged sleep. She could hear noise, voices, and realised that it must have been that which woke her.

Oh the opposite bunk Sophie stirred.

'Miss Tarrant, I'm so thirsty. May I have some water?' she said, plaintively.

Horror cleared Abigail's brain instantly. Dear God, she had been so exhausted that she had fallen asleep and whilst she had slept the train had stopped without her being aware of it.

Shakily she reached for the water bottle and shook it. It was empty. Getting unsteadily to her feet she lifted a corner of the blind, gasping as a wave of heat wafted into the small compartment. It was a little after dawn. By midday it would be unbearable, and they had no water. She struggled with fingers which seemed suddenly clumsy to free the blind. She had no idea when they would stop again.

In the confined space she managed to slip into her robe, then released the blind to lean out of the window. The platform was crowded with travellers, baggage coolies, and food vendors making their way along the length of the train, handing up dishes of food, mainly rice and heavily spiced meats. The smell rose to fill her nostrils as her gaze searched desperately among the crowd, then she saw the water vendor. At her signal he ambled towards her, a small man, his lined face swarthy beneath the white turban.

'*Tahsa char, garumi garum,*' he chanted. '*Pahn biri.*' She shook her head as cigarettes were thrust towards her.

'No, water. I need water.'

Another dish came. 'Very good *jellabies,* memsahib.'

Her stomach contracted at the sight of the fried sweets made of batter and honey.

'No, thank you, just water.'

To her relief the man took the bottle and filled it. Seeing the open doors of some of the carriages being closed Abigail hurriedly held out a handful of coins, and as he took one allowed her gaze to search the small station. It was like being part of a dream. How was it possible that she was here, in this place which was like an oasis in the midst of a desert, where the sun blazed down on rocks and arid sand and the air was heavy with the smell of dust and spices and other smells she had never encountered before.

The train was moving again and she drew back into the compartment, lowering the blind again before turning to

Sophie. 'Here, I have water, drink just a little. No, gently now.' She supported the child, brushing back the dark hair and was a little alarmed to see the pallor of the small face. She forced a smile as Sophie lay down again.

'Is that better?'

Sophie nodded but closed her eyes and didn't speak. Abigail sat beside her, holding the small hand in her own as she tried to quell the first ripples of panic. The journey had been a nightmare. First the sea crossing and then the endless train journey from Bombay. Sophie was exhausted but she couldn't be ill, she mustn't be. Releasing herself Abigail reached for the water, pouring a little on to her handkerchief. She lay it over Sophie's forehead and the child stirred restlessly. 'Will we soon be there? I'm tired and my head hurts.'

Abigail rose from the bunk to search for her bag. 'A few more hours, darling. In the meantime I have some cologne, perhaps that will help.' She dabbed a little on the burning skin, its fragrance momentarily wafting into the compartment. She watched as Sophie's eyes flickered open. 'When we reach Mandara you'll be able to sleep in a nice cool bed and you'll soon feel better. You've been very brave.'

The small mouth trembled suddenly. 'I don't want to go to Mandara. I didn't want to come to India. Why did I have to come? What if my father doesn't want me?'

To Abigail's dismay she began to sob uncontrollably. With a quick movement she gathered Sophie to her, holding her close yet afraid she would hear the pounding of her own heart. 'But of course he will want you. How can you even think such a thing?'

'But he doesn't know me.' Vehemence faded as sobs wracked the small body. 'Perhaps he will hate me as he hated my mother.'

'Hush now.' Abigail swallowed hard. 'It isn't true that he hated your mother.'

'It is true. I heard my aunt say it. He drove her out.'

Abigail shook her head. 'Sometimes things are not as they seem. We only know part of the story and things become confused.' She bit her lip. 'You'll see, in a little while you'll get to know one another and become friends. It will be a great adventure.' Above the lowered head she had to blink back her own tears.

'You'll stay with me, won't you Miss Tarrant?'

The question caught her unawares and her heart missed a beat. 'I . . . well of course I shall stay with you for a while, until you are settled in your new home.'

'It isn't my home, it isn't.' The dark eyes were wide and brilliant with tears.

Abigail had to force herself to speak. 'I know it isn't yet, dearest, but in a while, you'll see. You'll make lots of new friends. Do you remember all the people on board the ship, the children coming from their schools in England to be with their parents.'

Sophie released herself to lie back, turning her head against the pillow.

'But I'm not going to be with my parents. He isn't my father. I don't want him and he doesn't want me.' The words faded as she flung her arm across her face then turned away.

With a sigh Abigail returned to her own bunk where she sat feeling drained. The heat was even more oppressive and she pressed a hand to her face, wondering how anyone could ever grow used to something so cruel and unrelenting. She raised the blind now that the train was moving again, and stared out at the dry sandy wilderness. Did it breed those same qualities in the men who chose to live out here, she wondered, and shuddered involuntarily.

Lying down she closed her eyes trying to sleep, but it was useless. Finally she abandoned the attempt, getting up again to pour a little of the water into the basin, splashing it on to her face and throat. It was warm but she tilted her head back allowing the droplets to trickle over her skin. Her petticoat clung to her body but it would have to suffice since there was no room to unfasten the box which contained her clothes. Reluctantly she stepped into her gown. The high collar seemed to restrict her breathing as she fastened it and turned to a small, cracked mirror to study her reflection.

What she saw appalled her. In the ashen pallor of her face her eyes were made to seem large by the shadows beneath them. Her hair hung over her shoulders, tendrils clinging damply to her cheek. She brushed it, twining it into a coil at the nape of her neck, then she splashed a little of the cologne on to her temples and sat for a moment with her eyes closed. This offered no escape and she got up to look out of the window. Soon she would have to waken Sophie. Mandara drew closer but there could be no pleasure in the thought for either of them.

The station platform was crowded as they stood, surrounded by their trunks, Abigail's gaze searching anxiously in the hope that someone might have been sent to meet them. As the crowd gradually thinned the hope became remote, and she had to battle with the feelings of resentment which rose within her, as well as the growing anxiety. How was she to get herself and Sophie with all their luggage to Mandara?

It was obvious that many of the travellers were men returning to their units after taking leave. Their uniforms made brilliant splashes of colour in the drab, dusty surroundings. Abigail fanned her cheeks with a handkerchief, the gesture doing nothing to relieve the heat but at least keeping off the flies.

'Put your hat on, Sophie, dear,' she ordered. The child obeyed, her face flushed and sullen as she wandered away to sit on one of the larger trunks, her chin sunk on to her hands in a gesture so forlorn that Abigail felt a renewed anger against the man who could behave so shabbily. She bit her lip indecisively, wondering what to do, when a voice spoke from behind her and she turned, recognising one of the passengers whom she had met briefly on board ship.

'Miss Tarrant, isn't it?'

'Oh yes. Mr Peters.' She couldn't keep the relief from her voice as she stared up at the tall, slim figure. 'I hadn't realised you were travelling to Dilawar.'

A smile etched the lines deeper into his attractive face. 'Nor I you or I might have been of some assistance.' His gaze went beyond her to Sophie and returned, mildly curious. 'India is fine for those who know it but it can be pretty frightening for those who don't.'

She laughed, unaware as she did so, of the attractive picture she made, with her complexion already lightly tanned by the sun. 'Yes, I see what you mean.'

He drew her aside allowing a laughing group to pass, his hand lingering beneath her arm as she gazed enviously at a young woman carrying a parasol.

'I've just returned from a spot of leave myself. Couldn't wait to get back. Something about the smell of the place if you see what I mean.'

She nodded. Yes, she did know. It had been there, subtly, from the moment they had stepped ashore from the ship, the fragrant mixture of spices and flowers.

'Can't get used to the English climate,' he said. 'Not the same for the women of course.'

She looked at the near-deserted station. 'Your. . . wife. . .?'

'Stayed behind in England to see our daughter into school,' he offered. 'She'll join me later.' His glance flickered over her appreciatively. 'This is your first time out here.'

Her eyes widened. 'Is it so obvious?'

'Very.' His smile was attractive. 'But don't let it worry you. The truth is, after a while you get used to seeing the latest batches of young ladies who come out here for the express purpose of finding a husband.' Her shocked expression seemed to amuse him. 'There are those who are already married of course, who are coming out to join their husbands with their regiments or on a station somewhere. There are the fiancées too, but mostly they are the young hopefuls and most don't return home. It's the social order you see, very important out here. A man is expected to have a wife. It helps. Keeps things neat at the Colonel's lady's tea parties.' His teeth were very white against the dark tan. 'Have I shocked you?'

'No.' Her hand fluttered to her throat. 'Not at all. It's just that I hope no one will imagine that I. . .' Embarrassed colour flooded her face and he laughed.

'I'm sure they won't, Miss Tarrant, though they may be disappointed.'

His glance held hers for a long moment until she looked away, quickly.

'I'm afraid we seem to be stranded. I was sure we would be met. It's obviously all a misunderstanding.' She broke off, frowning. 'What does one do for transport out here?'

'That's no problem, though it rather depends on how

far you intend going. A *dak-ghari's* what you need. Not exactly stylish but serviceable. I'll arrange it.' He scanned the platform beckoning to a distant figure. 'Where exactly are you bound?'

'A place called Mandara. I'm sure you won't know it. . .' She broke off, startled by the sudden change in his expression as the smile died on his face.

'Mandara? Not the Farraday place?'

'Why, yes. That is, Mr Brett Farraday. But do you know him?'

His manner had suddenly become icily different. 'I have to admit that I do have that misfortune.'

Stunned, she stared up at him. 'I'm afraid I don't understand.'

His eyes searched her face, warily. 'You're not personally acquainted with Farraday I take it?'

She frowned, glancing quickly towards Sophie but the child was fortunately oblivious. 'No, we have never met, as a matter of fact.'

'Yet you come all this way, to Mandara?' It was almost as if he doubted her word and she drew back, resentfully.

'I am taking his daughter to him, that is my only connection with Mr Farraday.'

'His daughter?' The grey eyes widened incredulously. 'My God, you don't mean that that is his child?' There was suddenly a greyish tinge about his features as he stared at the small figure now wandering aimlessly along the platform, trailing her hat in one hand.

'Why, yes.' An icy hand gripped her. 'But I don't understand. What is wrong?'

The laughter on his lips somehow didn't reach his eyes. 'It's nothing.' He avoided her gaze, yet why, she wondered, should he suddenly become so guarded.

'You must forgive me, Miss Tarrant, perhaps I've already said too much. It was just a bit of a shock that's all. I mean, we've heard the talk, that he had a daughter, it's just that no one ever actually saw her.'

'No, well they wouldn't. She has lived in England until now, with her aunt.' She had to wait, impatiently, as he gave orders to a baggage coolie and their trunks were loaded aboard a wooden, horse-drawn wagon. But she persisted after he had lifted Sophie on to one of the seats, refusing to accept his help and facing him instead. 'Mr Peters please, you have implied that something is wrong. . .'

His mouth tightened. 'Look, Miss Tarrant, I'd be obliged if you just forgot anything I said.'

'But how can I do that?'

'I spoke out of turn that's all. It was nothing. I'll be happy to escort you to the perimeter of my own land, it borders Farraday's. But I'm not prepared to risk getting my head blown off by putting so much as a foot on his spread.'

She whitened. 'Getting your. . . but why should he wish to do such a thing?'

'Because he's a madman, Miss Tarrant.' Abruptly his hands spanned her waist and she was lifted off her feet and swung up into the wagon where she sat looking down at him. 'Look, I've warned you. If you take my advice you'll go back to England and take the child with you. She'll be better off there. Mandara's no place for either of you.'

She had to swallow hard to remove the sudden restriction in her throat. 'I'm afraid we can't do that. We don't have any choice.'

He stood looking up at her and for a moment she

almost thought it was fear she saw in his eyes. 'Then I'm sorry.'

She moved aside as he swung up beside her and though she longed to pursue the matter it wasn't possible with Sophie chattering. Eventually James Peters turned to stare in troubled silence out of the window.

They must have travelled for miles and the journey became a nightmare as the temperature rose still higher. Sophie mercifully fell asleep, but for Abigail there was no similar oblivion. She tried in vain to waft a little cool air on to her cheeks with her handkerchief, only to abandon the attempt and lie instead with her head back against the wooden seat. She felt limp and drained. Her gown was clinging to her and a rivulet of sweat ran down her back. It was almost a relief to see James Peters, who had until then seemed quite impervious to the discomfort, take out his own handkerchief to mop his brow.

'I'm afraid you've picked the worst time to come,' he said. 'The cool season ends in March. From now until the monsoons it just gets worse. Look,' he directed her gaze to the roof of the *dak-ghari* where she saw the blistered paintwork. 'Nothing lasts for long out here.'

Exhausted, she had to force herself to speak. 'Yet you come back.' She turned her head slowly to look at him. 'Just what is it that you do out here, Mr Peters?'

'James.'

She nodded.

'I'm with the Forest Service, like my father before me. It's the way things are out here, tradition. A man's father is with the army, his son finds himself in uniform without knowing how it happened. It's the same with everything else. The Indian Civil Service, forestry, tea, indigo.'

'And Mr Farraday, where does he fit into this system?'

In the rapidly fading light Abigail sensed rather than saw him tense again.

'Farraday is a law unto himself, Miss Tarrant. The common belief is that he doesn't know the meaning of the word "rules". He chooses not to conform.'

'But surely he must have some friends.'

'Any he might have had were driven away years ago. He prefers it that way and frankly he's welcome. There are standards to be maintained, even out here, *especially* out here, where a man depends on his neighbour for everything, his social life included.'

She didn't answer but turned to stare in silence at the passing landscape. Shadows were beginning to form and, in the far distance, a faint pink glow touched the sky, lighting up a jagged line of peaks which might have been a whole world away.

'Is Mr Farraday with the Forest Service too?'

'Good God, no. I thought you knew. Farraday owns a mine. Rubies.'

For some reason her heart changed its beat. 'Rubies?'

'It was the devil's own luck as a matter of fact. One of his workers just dug a stone out of a clump of earth about ten years ago.' Suddenly there was a hardness in his tone. 'They dug a seam and it was rich.' His laughter had a hollow ring to it. 'Whatever else you say about Farraday he has had luck, though much good it may have done him. They say it cost him his wife. I say he can take full credit for that himself.'

Abigail's hand tightened against her throat. Beneath the bodice of her gown she could feel the chain from which the ring given into her keeping was suspended. Suddenly the stone seemed to burn against her flesh.

The shadows had deepened when James Peters called out something to the driver of the *dak-ghari*. The vehicle came to a halt on the rutted track and he clambered down.

'This is the border of my land, Miss Tarrant. I'll walk from here. The boy will take you on.' He held out his hand, enclosed her fingers within it, retaining his hold. 'If you should ever wish, or need to come over to my place I hope you'll do so. I assure you it will all be perfectly proper. My sister is staying with me until Olivia joins me again.'

She withdrew her hand quickly. 'Thank you, I. . . I will remember, but it seems unlikely that we shall meet again. I expect to be returning to England very shortly.'

She told herself she had imagined the look of regret in his eyes as he stepped away and said something to the boy. Then the wagon began to move again and when she looked back, her hand raised in farewell, he had gone.

CHAPTER
TWO

ABIGAIL felt Sophie's hand tremble in hers as she stared up at the man bowing before her.

'Away? I don't understand. Mr Farraday can't be away.' She was aware that her voice was raised, tinged with alarm, but she couldn't prevent it. Exhaustion and uncertainty lent an air of frightening unreality to everything. In particular to the figure clad in white, whose face stared impassively from beneath the turban wound about his head. There was something about the swarthy features which gave her a feeling of unease. His manner was that of a servant yet she saw nothing of subservience in the piercing eyes which regarded her almost contemptuously. He had appeared as if from nowhere, so silently that she was still trembling, and she knew that beside her Sophie was close to tears. She drew herself up. 'We are expected. Mr Farraday must have received Lady Flixton's letter warning him of our arrival. Where is he? Let me speak to someone. . .'

The dark eyes narrowed. 'I am Gopal, memsahib, bearer to the Sahib Farraday. I regret that he is not here to greet you.

'But when will he be back?'

'Perhaps not for many hours, memsahib. I do not know.'

She bit back an angry retort. Though there had been no change in his expression, she sensed that he resented her intrusion, that he was savouring this small triumph over her frustration as she stood helplessly, staring about her, knowing she must do something, for Sophie's sake, yet unable to decide what. To her dismay she knew that no image she had conjured up of Mandara could ever have prepared her for the reality. After the heat it was like stepping into a cold shadow and she shivered involuntarily, her hand tightening about Sophie's. The hall in which they stood was edged by pillars and archways. The floor was tiled, making the sound of their voices echo against white walls on which many pictures hung. Her gaze took in carpets and hangings, things of beauty which should have enhanced the room, yet there was a coldness, as if sunlight had been for ever banished. From somewhere beyond one of the archways, there came the sound of water splashing gently, and a heady scent of flowers which made her feel dizzy and light-headed. She brushed a hand against her forehead, knowing that she must not faint, but everything seemed to be spinning around her. A staircase, vast and wide. Above it a gallery which seemed to encircle the vastness of the hall where they stood. So much beauty yet so cold. She felt breathless and it was with an effort that she managed to drag herself back to reality and face the bearer. She would not be intimidated.

'Perhaps you will be good enough to have us shown to our rooms. We are both very tired and hungry and I am sure that not even Mr Farraday would wish us to await his return without some refreshment.'

Some expression flickered over the dark face as the Indian bowed. 'It shall be done, memsahib.'

'I'm not hungry,' Sophie wailed. 'My head hurts.'

Indeed she did seem a little flushed.

'Is the little memsahib not well?'

'I think she has a slight fever though I hope it is

nothing serious. I'm sure all she needs is a good night's sleep.' She frowned down at Sophie. 'Perhaps we will excuse you a meal and just tuck you up in bed. I'm sure your father will understand, under the circumstances, if you are not able to see him until tomorrow.'

'I don't want to see him, ever.'

'Hush, my dear,' Abigail murmured, trying to control her anger against the man who hadn't afforded them even the courtesy of being there when his daughter arrived. Gathering up her bag she followed the bearer towards the stairs. 'I think Mr Farraday should be informed that his daughter is unwell even though I'm sure it is nothing serious. If you will tell him the moment he returns,' she said firmly.

Gopal paused, his gaze challenging hers. 'The sahib will be very tired. It is his custom not to be disturbed.'

Abigail clenched her hand against the urge to strike him. It was a battle of wills and one which, for Sophie's sake, she knew she must win. Lifting the hem of her skirts she began to climb the stairs. 'Tonight he will be disturbed, whether it is his custom or not. If you don't wish to do it then I shall see him myself.'

He was beside her and she sensed his enmity but she met it unflinchingly, and only as he inclined his head in silent acknowledgement did she release her breath. It had been a small victory, but as she saw his mouth clamped into a rigid line she knew that she was far from winning the battle.

She supported Sophie up the stairs and paused as he thrust open doors.

'The memsahib's rooms are prepared.'

She scarcely took in anything of her surroundings. Weariness was falling over her like a great, heavy blanket but she knew she could not postpone her meeting with

Brett Farraday any longer. No matter how late his return, she must be there.

'I will eat in an hour.' It was difficult to remember now when she had last had any food but her stomach felt empty.

Again, the merest inclination of his head before he turned to disappear on silent feet, leaving her to usher Sophie into the room. Immediately she began to help the child out of her clothes and slipped a nightgown over her head before helping her to climb in between the sheets. There were no other covers, merely a net hanging over the bed. Kissing Sophie she drew this down and stood looking at her as the child struggled against sleep.

'Do I have to see my father tomorrow, Miss Tarrant. I don't feel well.'

Abigail's eyes searched the small face, frowning. 'I dare say by morning, when you've had a good sleep, you'll feel differently, and you have to meet him some time you know. Do you really feel unwell?'

Sophie turned her head away. 'My head hurts, really it does.'

'Perhaps if you close your eyes.' She smoothed back the dark hair and watched as the lashes fluttered and finally closed. Sophie was asleep and, pray God, by morning Abigail would be proved right, that it was only rest she needed.

Making her way slowly to her own room which adjoined Sophie's, she unfastened her gown, slipping out of it to sit on the bed. The urge to lie down, just for a few moments, and close her eyes was intense, but she knew that to give in to it would be fatal. She would be asleep almost before her head touched the pillow and no matter how exhausted she felt she was determined she would put off a confrontation with Brett Farraday not a moment longer than she had to.

That he would not be here to receive them upon their arrival had simply not occurred to her, yet she chided herself now for not having expected it. What kind of man was he, she asked herself, angrily, that he could ignore even his own child?

She dressed with care in a gown of pale grey satin. For Sophie's sake she had abandoned the mourning, and the grey offered a compromise between her grief and the necessity of continuing with her own life. She studied her image in the glass. The lace collar hugged her throat and the skirts moulded to her waist and hips, but the colour seemed only to emphasise the pallor of her cheeks. With a grimace she turned away. What did it matter how she looked. It wasn't as if she had to impress Brett Farraday—even if he was capable of being impressed, which she doubted. She ran her fingers through her hair and began to brush it vigorously until all traces of dust had gone and it hung thick and soft again, then she coiled it, securing it with pins. After a few moments she made her way downstairs, pausing tentatively in the silence, wondering which way to go. As if at some signal Gopal appeared, though she was certain she had made no sound. His hand indicated that she should follow and she did so to discover that a meal awaited her in a room which overlooked a terrace lit by lamps.

She had imagined her appetite had deserted her until she sat at the table and food was put before her by a smiling servant who attended capably to her needs— filling her glass with wine, removing empty dishes. Though he spoke it was in his own native tongue and once again Abigail was aware of a sense of isolation.

Having eaten an exquisite mixture of meat, subtly

spiced and served with rice, followed by deliciously cool fruit, she sat back toying with her glass, listening to the night sounds and feeling a breeze stir the wisps of hair against her cheek. Her gaze went to the empty chair at the far end of the table and for one incredible moment it was as if she experienced the presence of someone there, watching her, proclaiming his right to be there and her own intrusion. Her fingers tightened on the stem of her glass and she thrust it away violently, spilling a few drops of the dark red liquid. It was only as she looked up sharply that she saw Gopal standing in the shadows and knew that he had been watching. Dipping her fingers into a small bowl of scented water she dabbed them dry on her napkin and rose to wander out on to the terrace. Anything to escape the presence which seemed to fill this house.

She breathed deeply, filling her lungs with air. Darkness had fallen, filling the night with strange sounds and scents and the sky was brilliant with stars. To her delight, as she made her way down a short flight of steps she saw a fountain, splashing into a pool. Staring into it she saw fish darting back and forth beneath the ripples. It was so unexpected that she smiled involuntarily—but then everything about Mandara was unexpected and left her feeling confused. There was so much beauty yet no one to appreciate it. Only Brett Farraday who chose to be master of all he surveyed in his own private little kingdom.

She shivered in spite of the warm night air. It was easy to see now what had driven Elaina away. It was like being trapped in a prison of silence. Yet how different it would be, to share all this beauty with the man one loved, to be together in such an exotic paradise.

The sound of footsteps behind her sent her whirling round and she felt the colour flood into her cheeks as she stared up into the face of the man who stood watching her. He began to move slowly towards her. She felt her heart begin to pound. How long had he stood there? She had the insane notion that he had been able to read her thoughts and despised her for them.

Her hands gripped the wall behind her as he came closer. He was tall and slim yet there was a ruggedness about him, a muscular strength which seemed to ripple beneath the open-necked shirt he wore. In the flickering light of the lanterns she saw the film of sweat gleaming at his tanned throat and she became aware of a pair of eyes studying her, coldly analytical, from beneath the shadow of dark eyebrows. He flicked a riding crop against the palm of his hand and she saw that he was dressed for riding in boots and breeches. Dust etched the lines of exhaustion more deeply into what was even so a handsome face.

She knew she should speak but her voice seemed to have fled her throat. Without a shadow of doubt she knew that this was Brett Farraday and, for no reason she could explain, she felt like an animal, trapped, able to do nothing but await the pleasure of its tormentor.

He came to a halt, towering above her and she was struck by the cruel sensuality of his mouth. His gaze raked her from head to toe before he turned contemptuously away, flinging the riding crop from him. 'Miss Tarrant, I take it?' She opened her mouth to speak but before she could do so his angry gaze had silenced her. 'Miss Tarrant, I've had a hard day, I'm tired and hungry so let's get one thing clear before you say a word. You are not welcome here. I didn't ask you to come and I intend to see to it that you and the child go back to England on the first ship available. Is that perfectly clear?'

Stunned, she could only stare, open-mouthed. She felt the anger welling up inside her but the suddenness, the coldness of his attack had taken her so unawares that she was bereft of speech. She was conscious of Gopal at his side. His look turned in her direction before he poured wine and retreated once more. It had been sufficient for her to guess his triumph and she knew that she was trembling.

Brett Farraday drained the glass in one, crossed to the decanter and, as she watched, filled it and drank again before dragging his gaze reluctantly towards her.

Somehow she managed to find her voice 'Mr Farraday.' Her voice sounded unlike her own.

He motioned the glass towards her. 'I may also tell you that I intend to get good and drunk so if it offends your precious morals I recommend that you leave now. In any case I'd be glad if you would do so. I don't care for company, Miss Tarrant, and in particular I don't care for yours.' He sank on to one of the chairs. 'Gopal!' The bearer appeared, bowing. 'Bring me some food and for God's sake help me off with these damned boots.'

The bearer did so, easing them off, then saying, 'The sahib shall eat at once.' He clapped his hands as he moved away and she heard him issuing orders.

Abigail stood, her hands clenched together, feeling as if what until that moment had been a dream had suddenly become a nightmare. Brett Farraday looked up, his mouth curling sardonically.

'What's the matter? Have I shocked you, Miss Tarrant?'

'No.' She almost choked on the word and he laughed softly as he rose to his feet.

'You're not a very good liar Miss Tarrant, but then, I doubt you've had much practice. I've upset your pretty notions of what is proper, you've decided I'm an ill-mannered oaf—and you're right.' His mouth twisted savagely. 'By God you're right and if you're expecting an apology, forget it. I've never apologised for anything in my life and I don't intend to start now, especially to a woman.'

Abigail's knees were shaking and she knew that were she to release her hold on the wall she would fall, yet somehow she must put some distance between herself and the unbelievable arrogance of this man. He was utterly contemptible, far worse than anything she had dared to expect, and she felt sick at the thought of leaving Sophie to his tender mercies.

She forced herself to look at him. 'I don't ask for an apology, Mr Farraday. I realise that to do so would be a waste of time. I see you have no notion whatsoever of what is decent.'

'Well I'm glad you appreciate that. It saves a lot of time and awkwardness.'

She bit her lip, tasting the blood though she was aware of no pain. 'I assure you, Mr Farraday, that your unwillingness to have me here is far surpassed by my own unwillingness to remain a moment longer than is absolutely necessary for me to do so.' His eyes surveyed her above the rim of his glass and she heard the tremor in her voice. 'But since I was given little choice in this matter and as you were informed of our arrival, I should have thought you might at least have had the courtesy to be here when we arrived.'

His glass was lowered with such anger that she flinched. 'Yes, I was *informed* of your arrival, Miss Tarrant. Unfortunately the letter arrived too late for me to do anything about it otherwise I would most certainly have taken steps to prevent your coming here. As for my not being here to greet you, I doubt whether it will be of any interest to you, but I lost one of my workers today, a good man, killed because someone has decided they don't like my being here.'

Her face paled. 'I. . . I'm sorry of course.'

'Sorry.' He looked at her, disbelief mirrored in the grey eyes. He refilled his glass again. 'Look, I don't know why you've come and I'm not interested. There's nothing for you here and the sooner you get back to England and take the child with you, the better.'

She swallowed hard. 'We got here only a few hours ago, Mr Farraday. We are tired, very tired, but I repeat, nothing would induce me to remain a moment longer than is necessary, but surely you cannot mean to refuse to see your daughter?'

He uttered an oath with such violence that she had to summon every ounce of her courage not to turn and run. 'My daughter? And whose word have I that she is mine, Miss Tarrant? Yours?'

She had struck him even before she knew what she intended. She watched with rapt fascination as the red weal spread across his face, then suddenly her wrist was caught in a vice-like grip and she cried out. She struggled but he merely held her more firmly, his fingers burning against her skin. He was close, menacingly close, and she could scarcely breathe.

'You are contemptible.' She flung the words at him but the dark eyes were without remorse.

'I doubt that you knew my wife, Miss Tarrant. If you had you'd know that just because she said it, doesn't make it so.'

She stared in shocked disbelief. 'How can you say that? You haven't seen the child. If you had you couldn't doubt.' She realised that it was true. She had imagined

Sophie resembled her mother but she saw in this man the same eyes, the same mouth, the same colouring.

He thrust her away. 'You're remarkably naive, Miss Tarrant. Even if it was true, the child was never mine in reality. We are strangers and it's best it stays like that. I don't need more complications in my life. Just get her out, keep her away from me.' He brushed a hand through his hair and the shadows deepened the lines of exhaustion in his face as he turned away.

Unthinkingly she lifted her hand only to let it fall again. It couldn't be pity she was feeling, not for this man—and yet something had for one incredible moment made her want to reach out, to touch him, to brush the dark hair from his brow . . . Her voice shook, 'Sophie needs you. She has no one else. Is it so inconceivable that perhaps you need her too?'

His head rose and the stark expression in his eyes shocked her. 'And just what do you base all this superior knowledge on, Miss Tarrant?' The cold glance mocked her. 'It is *Miss* Tarrant isn't it?' He caught her wrist and forced her fingers open. 'There's no ring so there's no man and yet you think you know me.'

Her fingers clenched within his grasp. 'I simply didn't fall in love. Is that a crime?'

'Love.' His laughter was brutal. 'And just what do you think love is? I'll tell you, it's nothing. It's a game women play but at heart they are all cheats.' He drew her relentlessly closer, then his hand was beneath her chin, forcing her to look at him. She closed her eyes as a sense of weakness gripped her and she became conscious of the sinewy strength of his body against hers. 'And you are the worst kind of all, Miss Tarrant.' His voice was cold as ice against her cheek. 'You look so innocent but you're not. It's all part of the trap.'

She tried to pull away but his hands held her like steel bands. 'No. . .' She tried to turn her head away but he jerked her closer still and before she knew what he intended his mouth had closed ruthlessly upon hers. She tried to fight him but it was as if a fire coursed through her body. He held her, her body crushed against him, and the more she struggled the more violently he held her, his lips bruising her mouth. She had no strength to fight him and, suddenly, no desire to be free. Her senses reeled and she submitted weakly, returning the kiss. It was madness, utter madness. For a second she felt his body tense as her mouth softened beneath his, then she was free. With an oath he had thrust her away and, stunned, she almost fell. Her heart was racing so madly that she felt as if it would burst. Then she opened her eyes and found him looking at her, his mouth twisted with contempt.

'You see,' he drawled. 'Cheats, all of you.'

'Why you. . .' She pressed a hand to her mouth as if it were possible to erase the pressure of his lips. 'You are despicable.'

'Really? I had the strangest feeling that you enjoyed it, Miss Tarrant, so what does that make you?'

A cry died in her throat as she tried to speak and couldn't. He was right, she had enjoyed it, but now shame flooded through her like a wave. How could she have behaved in such a way? So cheaply? Blindly she turned and ran up the steps and into the hall, almost stumbling over the hem of her gown. Her feet echoed on the tiled floor as she ran towards the stairs. Vaguely she was aware of Gopal, emerging from the shadows. For one brief moment their glances met before she fled past him. Somehow she managed to reach the safety of her room where she flung herself on to the bed and lay

breathing hard, her fingers coiled tightly in the coverlet.
She hated Brett Farraday. He was arrogant, coarse and
brutal. But most of all, the thought came unbidden, she
was afraid of the power he had had over her which had
robbed her of the will to resist.

She lay for a long time before the anger faded, then
she sat up and tugged at the pins which held her hair,
letting it fall against her shoulders. She had to get away
from Mandara as soon as possible. There was no longer
any real purpose in her remaining. She had delivered
Sophie to her father and her responsibility was ended.
But was it? Could she really escape so easily? Now more
than ever she feared for the child. How could she predict
what a man like Brett Farraday might do?

Her fingers trembled against her lips. No man had
ever kissed her in such a way before. Suddenly she was
confused, afraid of the sensations it had aroused in
her—yet to Brett Farraday it had all been part of a game.
In an attempt to escape her thoughts she got up from the
bed and brushed her hair, then took off her gown and
slipped into her nightgown and a thin robe. She was
exhausted. It seemed like days rather than hours since
she had arrived yet, maddeningly, the desire to sleep had
gone. The air was stiflingly heavy and she wondered if
Sophie was asleep.

Fastening her robe she made her way to the child's
room to find her tossing restlessly beneath the mosquito
net. The little face was filmed with sweat. Anxiously
Abigail dipped a cloth into a jug of water to bathe the
flushed cheeks then she frowned, trying to stifle a pang
of alarm. This was no natural sleep. The child had a
fever.

She stood for several minutes looking down at her.
She had to get help, yet the mere thought of seeing Brett

Farraday again was more than she could bear. Biting her lip she moved to the door and as she opened it, saw rather than heard Gopal coming up the stairs. Revulsion rose within her and she drew back, hesitating even whilst knowing she had little choice.

'The memsahib wishes something? The maid will unpack. . .'

'No, I. . . I think Miss Farraday is unwell. I noticed it when we left the ship but thought she was merely over-tired. Now. . . I don't know what to do.'

At this admission some merest flicker seemed to cross the Indian's face. 'If the memsahib wishes I will go to the little one.'

She glanced at the door, still wary, then looked at him. 'You?'

'I have some knowledge of fevers.'

Could she, dare she trust him? He resented their being there, how could she be sure? But almost as if he had sensed what was in her mind he said softly, 'If the memsahib wishes, I will inform the sahib.'

'No.' She flung out a hand to stop him. 'No, I have no wish to disturb him unless it should prove necessary.' She drew back towards the door. 'If you will tell me what needs to be done, I will do it.'

He followed her into the room and looked down at the sleeping child. He touched her cheek and neck gently. 'There is fever but not yet cause for concern. Sometimes it goes as quickly as it comes. The little memsahib needs sleep. By morning we shall know, not before.'

She stared at him, 'You mean we can do nothing? But what if she grows worse?'

The dark eyes studied her. 'Gopal will keep watch. The memsahib also needs sleep. It has been a long day, a long journey.'

It was true, she brushed a hand against her brow, and knew she was trembling both with exhaustion and re-action. The last thing she wanted was to become ill herself. 'Yes, I am very tired. If you are sure. . .'

'Quite sure, memsahib. I will keep watch.'

For some reason the words reassured her and she made her way slowly back to her room. The doors which led on to the balcony were open and she stepped out, staring up at the sky, brilliant with stars. She eased the tension at the back of her neck and shoulders, and as she did so she became aware of the solitary figure below.

Brett Farraday sat alone, an empty bottle on the table beside him, a glass in his hand. There was something about him, about the stillness of him, that made her breath catch in her throat. Then she realised that he was looking up at her and with a start she drew back quickly into the room, closing the doors behind her. For no reason she could explain she crossed quickly to the door and turned the key in the lock. She stared at it then laughed at herself for the gesture, after all, what reason had she to be afraid? Certainly not Brett Farraday who had made his contempt for her only too plain—for her, for all women. . . Her hand hovered but she left the key turned in the lock and finally went to bed to lie staring up at the net above her. It seemed to close her in, like a prisoner.

CHAPTER
THREE

'MEMSAHIB, memsahib!'

Abigail awoke suddenly, aware of someone tapping at the door. She sat up but it was some seconds before her befuddled brain could make any sense of what she heard or where she was. Then, as memory returned, she pushed aside the net and reached for her robe, hurrying to unlock the door. She had no idea how long she had slept. She had told herself she would just close her eyes and perhaps doze, but she realised with a sense of shock that it was daylight and the room was already filled with a dry heat.

She opened the door and Gopal stood there. Her gaze flew to his face, then to the door of Sophie's room and a feeling of panic rose. 'She is worse?'

'I fear so, memsahib.'

She fastened her robe and ran, neither knowing nor caring whether he followed. She went straight to the bed, drawing in her breath sharply as she looked down at Sophie.

'It is as I feared,' Gopal spoke quietly beside her. 'The fever has grown stronger.'

'But will she be all right?' Desperately she appealed to him, only to see the features inscrutable as ever.

'I cannot say, memsahib. The little one is young and sometimes the young have not the strength with which to fight.'

Appalled she dragged her gaze back to the hot little

face, watching helplessly as Sophie flung herself restlessly across the bed. 'We must do something. Sophie,
Sophie my dear.' The child's lashes flickered briefly as
she stared at Abigail only to close her eyes again. 'She
doesn't know me.'

'It is the way with the fever. It fights for possession of
the body.'

'But why didn't you call me sooner?' She turned to
Gopal violently only to find his gaze fixed calmly on her.

'The memsahib was exhausted after her journey and
needed sleep.'

'But we can't just leave her like this. There must be
something, medicine?' Her hand caught at his sleeve but
he shook his head.

'No, memsahib. No medicine. There is nothing to be
done but to wait and watch.'

Her eyes widened with disbelief. 'You can't mean
that. She's only a child. She hasn't the strength to fight.
Are you asking me to believe that she may die and we
can do nothing?' His complacency sickened her.

His brow furrowed. 'I have seen it happen many
times.'

'Well, I will not let it happen.' She shook her head,
fiercely. 'I won't, do you understand? I don't accept that
nothing can be done.' She heard the note of hysteria in
her voice but could do nothing to prevent it as she
rounded on him. 'I don't believe you want her to live.
You don't want us here, intruding upon your domain,
that's it, isn't it?' She was breathing hard, her eyes
brilliant with accusation, but still he faced her without
any hint of remorse.

'The memsahib is overwrought.'

Her hands clenched together. 'Yes, the memsahib *is*
overwrought, but not hysterical.'

'I do not think it, memsahib,' he said, quietly, but she ignored it.

'Mr Farraday must be sent for. He will know what is to be done. I insist that he is made aware of his responsibility.'

'That won't be necessary.'

She whirled as the voice came from behind her to see the tall figure standing in the doorway. A feeling of relief flooded through her, then died as his glance reminded her that she was still wearing only a thin robe over her nightgown. Instinctively she drew it more closely around her, feeling the colour rise to her cheeks, but he had already dismissed her from his thoughts as he strode to the bed and stared down at his daughter.

She saw a nerve twitch in his jaw and wondered what emotion he felt, if he was capable of any. Was it his wife he saw there? Did he feel any kind of guilt? She saw the knuckles of his hand gleaming white against the tan yet his face revealed nothing.

Unable to bear the silence any longer she said, 'We must do something. We can't just let her die. Gopal says there is nothing. . .'

'He is right.' He turned to face her and once again she had to fight off the strange sensations his nearness aroused. At least his coldness made it easier.

Her blue eyes stared at him, uncomprehending. 'I don't believe you.'

'I'm afraid you have no choice. The truth may seem very hard to you, Miss Tarrant, but Gopal is right. The fever will take its course and there is nothing you or I or anyone can do.'

She was shaking with anger as she faced him. 'Don't you care? Have you no feelings? Have you been shut away for so long that nothing reaches you any longer?'

She heard the soft hiss of his breath before he caught her wrist and, in spite of her cry of protest, propelled her with steel-like force from the room. She struggled and fought to free herself but to no avail and suddenly she was afraid. He flung open a door and thrust her inside, closing it before he released her.

She had been afraid of him last night but now she sensed that he was far more dangerous as he barred her escape, pacing back and forth like a caged animal, watching her as if not trusting himself to speak.

Her fingers clutched warily at the chair which had broken her fall. Instinctively she put it between them, knowing full well that it offered no real protection against this stranger. She forced herself to speak.

'You have no right—'

'I have every right.' She flinched as his fist crashed against the table yet he seemed to feel no pain. 'You are the intruder here. I am the master. The sooner you accept that the better, and don't ever think to challenge me or my authority again, especially in front of my servants. Is that clear?'

She tried to speak but her voice seemed to be trapped in her throat and she remained silent as he moved closer. 'I said is that clear, Miss Tarrant?'

Her chin rose and she forced herself to meet his gaze directly. 'Your daughter may be dying, yet you talk of authority? What kind of man are you, Mr Farraday. Are you made of ice?'

It was a mistake, she knew it as his brows drew together. Her cheeks flamed and she pressed a hand to her mouth expecting retaliation, but it didn't come. Clenching his fists he turned away and for the first time she could study him properly in the full light of day. Her heartbeat quickened. He was even more handsome than she had imagined the night before, yet now she saw the ruthlessness etched about his mouth. His black hair curled against the collar of his shirt and she noticed the patches of sweat darkening the fabric against his back.

'Just what is it that you want from me, Miss Tarrant?'

The question took her by surprise. 'Just some sign that you care. Is it too much to ask?'

His mouth was a grim line. 'Death is a fact of life out here.'

'It may be to you but not to me, not to Sophie. She is a child. She knows nothing of your way of life. She has been here for only a few hours.'

'That's all it takes. It comes with the ships. It's in the dust, the heat.'

'And you accept it?'

'Because I have no choice.'

'Or because it is easier,' she challenged swiftly and saw his head jerk upwards. 'Are you sure you haven't simply lost the will to fight, Mr Farraday? That is what takes the real courage.'

He had moved away and she couldn't see his expression, she merely heard the cold uninterest in his voice.

'You don't know what you're talking about, Miss Tarrant. Who gives you the right to judge me or my way of life? What is any of it to you?'

Yes, she thought, wearily, what was it to her? What did she care? But, irrationally or not, she did. 'Sophie gives me the right. I care what happens to her. She is your child. You have only to look at her to see it. You do see, yet you refuse to accept it. But why? Where does she belong if not with you?'

'Goddammit, not here,' he said, savagely. 'Not with me. My life suits me just the way it is, Miss Tarrant, and I've no intention of allowing you or that child to change it. The minute she is well enough, you get her out of here. Is that clear?'

Abigail didn't move. Every fibre of her being seemed to be alive with a burning anger. Or was it pity? He seemed to have the power to confuse her emotions. A deep shudder convulsed her body as she pulled away from him.

'One thing you have made very clear, Mr Farraday. I was right, it isn't blood you have in your veins it is ice and I see now only too clearly what your wife must have suffered. You are inhuman. Mandara is everything to you, there is no room in your life for anything or anyone else and so you drive them all away. I just wonder what it is that you are so afraid of.' Dimly she was aware of his face, a white blur before her, before she stumbled towards the door and fled.

For a long time after gaining the safety of her room she paced back and forth, surprised to find that she was still actually shaking from the encounter. Standing at the window she felt the heat against her skin as she saw Mandara in daylight for the first time since her arrival. It was odd that something could be so beautiful and at the same time so desolate, she thought, letting her gaze wander from the courtyard below, with its carefully nurtured plants and brilliant blooms, to the high, stone wall which was all that separated them from the hot, dry barrenness beyond. Had it been built to keep something out, she wondered, or something in? Had Elaina felt imprisoned by it, just as she did now?

She washed in the cool water which had been brought to her room, then chose her coolest gown. Her movements were lethargic as she stepped into it, not even aware that it was particularly attractive, the dark green colour complementing her skin and hair. Her brain was racing. She was conscious of only one thought, of getting away. She paused, looking around the room. Most of her belongings were still packed in the large trunk, apart from the few personal items which she had needed since her arrival. What was to stop her repacking them this very minute and returning to Bombay? She had her return ticket. The ship might not even have sailed yet.

But even as she thought it she knew it was impossible. While Sophie was ill she had no choice but to stay, and after that. . . It was something she couldn't bear to think about.

An image of arrogant features swam into her mind and she remembered the savagery of his kiss. She closed her eyes tightly but it refused to be banished and she clenched her hands. How was it possible that such a man could rouse these feelings of love and hate? With a sense of shame she recalled the willingness with which she had responded to him. In the mirror her cheeks flamed and she turned from it, pressing her hands to her face. Brett Farraday was utterly ruthless. She had accused him of being made of ice and it was true. Her fingers closed about the stone she wore on the chain at her neck. He was like the very gems he tore from the earth, cold and brittle. The sun caught the stone, sending out shafts of brilliant light like fire and she tore it from her neck, flinging it on to the dressing table. He was dangerous but she had no intention of getting burned.

Moments later she heard the sound of a horse being led into the courtyard below the terrace and, as if her thoughts had somehow conjured him up, she caught a brief glimpse of Brett Farraday as he climbed into the saddle. He exchanged some brief words with Gopal, controlling the stallion with ease as it shifted restlessly beneath him. Then he swung away, galloping out through the gates, looking like the devil, she thought, with the dark hair falling over his brow and his face wild as thunder.

When he had gone Gopal stood for a moment before turning to re-enter the house. She had the feeling that he was aware of her but if so he gave no sign of it. She might have been a ghost, Abigail thought. Like that of the dead woman who seemed to haunt this house and everyone in it.

A tapping sound at the door brought her back to reality and as she turned, a girl entered carrying a tray. She was so strikingly beautiful that Abigail found herself staring as the sari-clad figure moved gracefully towards her.

'*Chota hazri*, memsahib.' She set the tray down and bowed, pressing her long slender hands together. Abigail stared at the tea and fruit and realised that she hadn't yet eaten, but her interest was distracted as she stared with fascination at the delicately coloured skin which was neither Indian nor English. She held her breath, feeling a pang of envy, and was suddenly conscious of the disturbingly cool gaze which took in the comparative drabness of her own English gown and neatly coiled hair. This girl's features were perfection, framed by long, jet black hair. The mouth was sensual but it was the eyes which held her, for within their beauty was also something else. It was an expression Abigail couldn't read but, defensively, she moved into the shadows of the room and as she did so the girl smiled.

'The sahib gave orders that you were not to be woken after your journey, memsahib, but now he insists that you must eat.'

'Oh does he indeed? How very typical of him.' She purposely ignored the tray. 'I haven't seen you before.'

'No, memsahib. I am Gita.'

'Gita. It is a very pretty name. You speak very good English.'

Dark lashes veiled the lovely eyes. 'My father was British, memsahib. He came with the army to Udaipur where he met my mother.'

'How romantic.' Abigail knew that she had failed to keep the note of surprise out of her voice and felt suddenly uncomfortable as the girl's proud head rose.

'Not romantic, memsahib. My mother was very beautiful and very young but being also very foolish she believed the lies the British officer spoke to her, only to discover when he had shamed her in the eyes of her family that he no longer had any use for her.'

Abigail felt the colour drain from her face. 'Oh, I'm sorry.' She was conscious of the inadequacy of the words yet it was as if in some way her discomfiture amused the girl. 'You must not judge the actions of all men by those of one British officer.'

The lovely eyes held hers for a long moment before shifting to the balcony and something beyond which only she could see. 'I do not.'

'Surely your father was obliged to make some provision for you?'

'No, there was no provision. After all, what was my mother's word against the honour of the great British army? When she asked for him she was told he had gone away. They said many women came with such stories in the hope of being given money. She was big with child but she stayed to hear no more.'

Abigail felt sick. 'I don't understand.'

Gita poured the tea. 'There is no reason why the memsahib should understand. You are white and English. For me there is a barrier never to be crossed. I am neither British or Indian. I belong nowhere. I am despised.'

‗But that can't be true. Mr Farraday does not despise you.'

‘Ah no.' The words fell softly and a smile touched the lovely mouth. ‘But the sahib is not as other men. He also belongs nowhere, except here.' Her hands rose, the wrists encircled by bracelets. ‘Only at Mandara can he shut out the world and be as he truly is . . . until now.' She broke off and for a moment Abigail was afraid of the expression she saw glittering in the dark eyes which looked directly into hers. It was some seconds before she recognised a warning—a threat almost, but why? As if a cold hand had touched the nape of her neck, she shivered. She opened her mouth to speak but Gita moved quickly, pressing her hands together before she sped silently away.

Abigail felt as if her limbs were frozen. She must have been mistaken. What possible reason could there be for Gita to see her as any kind of threat? It made no sense, but the feeling of unease remained with her as she moved along the gallery towards Sophie's room.

What possible kind of threat could she offer to a girl she didn't know? She had been there for just one day, yet already Mandara seemed to have caught her within its web, and it was holding her prisoner.

CHAPTER
FOUR

FOR the next three days Abigail sat beside Sophie's bed, the hours interminable as she watched in vain for some sign of improvement, made worse by the heat and her anxiety. Reluctantly she allowed herself to be relieved of her duty, but only for a few hours when she returned to her own room, not to sleep properly but to doze, then to return, drugged by weariness, to her vigil. Food was brought to her on a tray. She ate mechanically, not even aware of who brought it or what she ate, aware only of the fact that Brett Farrraday had not once come to see his daughter.

And then, within the last few hours, the fever had worsened and she had refused to leave even as darkness fell. Gopal had tried to pursuade her but she had sent him away until, against her will, her own exhaustion had taken its toll and several times she had fallen asleep in her chair, only to waken suddenly as Sophie stirred. She got out of the chair to soak a cloth and lay it across the sweat-filmed brow, waiting expectantly for the lashes to flicker. But it didn't happen.

How much longer could it go on, she asked herself, easing her back as she crossed to the window. Already it was another new day, the sky was tinged with the first pink flush of dawn as it heralded the beginning of a further vigil.

She scraped her hair back from her forehead and opened the buttons at the neck of her gown. The day was at its coolest now, there was even a faint breeze. Pushing aside the gauzy curtains she leaned her head back letting it waft over her, heavy with the scent of flowers and spices. In another hour the sun would be glaringly hot and though she longed for sleep she knew it would be impossible.

She returned to her chair and the next thing she knew was when Gopal touched her arm. She jerked upwards with a cry of alarm.

'Oh, you startled me.'

'The memsahib needed sleep.'

'Sleep?' She blinked, then consternation filled her eyes as he drew back the curtains letting in the full glare of daylight.

'Oh no!' With a cry of distress she rose to her feet. How could she have allowed herself to fall asleep.

'The little memsahib has come to no harm.' Gopal followed her anxious gaze. 'There has been no change.'

Abigail bent, stiffly, to see for herself, but it was true. She pressed a hand to the child's cheek, listened to the shallow breathing. No, there had been no change either for the better, or, mercifully for the worse, but she would never forgive herself, even though relief surged through her.

She straightened up, aware that her gown was crumpled and her hair had come loose of its pins. A wave of dizziness seized her and she reached out blindly. Beads of sweat clung to her brow and Gopal's voice came to her as if from a great distance.

'The memsahib must rest, you cannot go on like this without sleep and food.' He held her as she gripped his arm, fighting against the fog which seemed to be clouding her brain.

'I will rest later.' Her mouth was incredibly dry.

'When Sophie is out of danger.' She stared at him but his face was just a blur.

'It may be many hours.'

'Yes, I know.' She pressed a hand to her head. 'But someone must keep watch. I must be here in case. . . in case she wakes and asks for me.'

'Then I shall watch.'

'You?'

'I give you my word, if the little one wakes, even for a moment, Gita will bring word. It will do no good if the memsahib should also become sick.'

Incredibly, she saw concern in his dark eyes but still she hesitated. How could she be sure he was to be trusted? But he was right. She looked at Sophie, of what use would she be to anyone if she became ill too?

'Perhaps I will lie down just for an hour.'

The Indian's gaze was direct, seeing the flush in her cheeks. 'The sahib will be most displeased. When he discovered you sleeping it was his intent to carry you to your room then. Only because he was certain the mem-sahib would be angry did he not do so. Instead he ordered that you be wakened in one hour, when he had left, and I am to tell you that it is his order that you rest properly.'

Her cheeks flamed. 'You mean. . . Mr Farraday was here, in this room?'

The slight inclination of Gopal's head confirmed it and her fists clenched in dismayed frustration. He had been here, had watched her while she slept, and she had not known it.

'And where is he now?'

'The sahib rode out at dawn.'

So she could not even excuse her lack of diligence to him. Blindly she turned and made her way to her own room where she lay on the bed, not even bothering to remove her gown. She stared up through the net, wishing it could shut out the images which seemed to crowd into her weary brain—the face of Brett Farraday. She turned her head away, closing her eyes, not to sleep but just to rest so that she would hear if they called. Her lashes fluttered, she sighed and slept at last.

For how long she slept it was impossible to say. She didn't know what woke her. For an instant it was as if something had brushed lightly against her cheek. A moth perhaps, or a breeze. Her eyelids felt heavy, as if she was waking from a drugged sleep and it was some moments before memory returned. When it did she sat up quickly, swinging her feet to the floor only to find that the room began to spin and she was obliged to sit, a hand pressed to her forehead, until it began to subside once again. What was wrong with her? She must get back to Sophie.

'Are you always so damnably stubborn, Miss Tarrant?'

The voice brought her up with a jerk and her horrified gaze rose to meet that of Brett Farraday as he lounged nonchalantly against the door. Conscious that yet again he had caught her unawares, her hand went to her hair, she was miserably aware of its disorder as his gaze seemed to mock her futile attempts.

'How long have you been here? What are you doing in my room?' Angrily she rose to her feet.

'Long enough to know you are exhausted. I didn't intend waking you.'

'You didn't. . .' Her voice faded as she remembered the moth against her cheek—had it perhaps been a hand? She stared at him then thrust the thought away.

No, it couldn't have been. Her hands fumbled awk-wardly at the buttons of her gown, refastening them as he watched. 'I didn't mean to fall asleep. I only closed my eyes. . .'

'Don't apologise,' he said roughly, moving towards her out of the shadow. She sensed that he was angry and her defences rose as he stood watching her. 'It isn't necessary for you to spend your every waking hour with the child. There is nothing you can do.'

'But you are wrong.' Her eyes widened as she flung the challenge at him. 'I can be there if. . . when she wakes.'

'There are servants.'

'Yes, there are servants, but they are also strangers, or doesn't that matter to you? When Sophie opens her eyes I want her to see a face she knows.'

He looked at her sharply. 'Meaning not mine.'

'No!' she bit back a cry of exasperation. 'No, that isn't what I meant. Oh why must you twist my words? On the contrary, I believe you should be there but since that isn't. . .', she swallowed hard. 'I'm sorry, I realise I have no authority here but I believe my place is with Sophie.' Her gaze flew up to meet his. 'Please, I beg you, allow me this.'

He moved impatiently. 'There is no need to beg. I can't forbid you to do as you please and even if I did,' his eyes raked her, 'would you obey me, Miss Tarrant?'

She pondered the question and met his gaze with determination. 'I want only what is best for Sophie. Can't you see,' her hand rose to plead with him, 'she needs her father. . .'

His eyes flashed a warning. 'Don't lecture me, damn it.'

He moved so sharply that she had to turn to follow him. 'It isn't my intention to lecture. The only thing I want is to make you see the truth.'

'The truth as *you* see it.'

She stood still, her head lowered as he paced back and forth. 'As you say, it is as I see it.' Her chin rose as she forced herself to look at him, to meet the steely gaze. 'What are you so afraid of, Mr Farraday? That if you lower your guard even for one moment you might actually find yourself caring for her? Would that truly be so terrible?'

He took a sharp breath, his face tightening, and she knew she had gone too far. Trembling she waited, expecting the explosion of anger to reach out and consume her. Miraculously, it didn't come. His mouth twisted contemptuously as he studied her. 'You have some fancy notions, Miss Tarrant. Well I'm sorry to disappoint you but my motives, I can assure you, are strictly basic. I don't need any added complications in my life. I don't need you, I don't need the child and what I said still goes, the minute she is well enough to travel, you take her back to England, is that clear?'

She pressed her quivering lips together. 'I refuse to believe you can be so heartless.'

'Well then you don't know me at all, Miss Tarrant, otherwise you would realise that nothing gets in my way, nothing and no one, unless I choose.'

Abigail felt the blanching of her skin. 'Do you always get what you want?'

'If I want it badly enough.'

In spite of her determination to remain calm, Abigail shivered. She tried to drag her eyes from his but they held her and she was aware of the tiny darts of fear, mingled with other emotions she refused to recognise, tingling through her body. He was arrogant and totally aware of his own strength, his male superiority.

'Then I pity you, Mr Farraday,' she thrust swiftly, 'For so far it appears you have very little.'

She didn't move as she said it but suddenly she was aware of him behind her, so close that she could feel the warmth of his breath on her neck, the heat of his body. He had only to reach out. Without warning a tremor ran through her. Fire stirred in her veins even as she told herself that this was utter madness. How could she want a man like Brett Farraday? She hated him for what he had done to one woman and for what he meant to do to his own child.

She heard the sharp intake of his breath before his hand came down on her shoulder, spinning her round to face him. Her eyes widened, startled, as she looked into his face, saw the grim line of his mouth.

'You're going too far, Miss Tarrant, and I warn you, it isn't wise.'

A sob caught in her throat. No, it wasn't wise. She was shocked by the responses of her own body to his touch. With a sharp cry she twisted violently, freeing herself from his grasp in an attempt to put some distance between them. Somehow she must fight this madness which could lead to nothing but misery and pain. He had made it all too clear that there was no room in his life for any other woman. Whatever had happened between himself and Elaina, somehow the dead woman still seemed to hold some kind of power over him.

She was breathing hard as she turned to face him and saw the pulse throb in his neck. For one brief moment some strange expression flickered in his eyes, something she couldn't read yet which she sensed meant danger. In the silence which hung between them her heart beat so loudly that she was sure he must hear it. What was happening to her? She took a frightened breath and it was as if the slight sound broke some spell. He moved abruptly, swearing softly under his breath as he crossed to the door.

'For pity's sake,' his voice came thickly, 'get some food. You look like a half-starved kitten and the last thing I need is another invalid.' He held the door open. 'I can't prevent you sitting with Sophie but at least I can make damned sure you have a proper break. From now on you'll get Gopal or one of the other servants to take a turn, is that understood?'

She tried to speak but couldn't. Instead she nodded, then, as he made to leave, 'But what about you, Mr Farraday, will you be visiting Sophie?'

She saw his hand tighten but he gave no other acknow-ledgement that he had even heard and she flinched as the door banged to a close behind him.

Having washed in tepid water from the pitcher left in her room, Abigail changed into a fresh gown of oyster satin and brushed and re-coiled her hair before making her way downstairs to where a meal was already awaiting her. The master, she observed, had wasted no time in making his orders known.

When she sat down, however, her appetite seemed to desert her so that she merely toyed with the food put before her. It looked delicious and she told herself she should try to eat in order to keep up her strength, but suddenly the very thought of food seemed to choke her. Tears pricked at her eyes and she blinked them away, furious with herself for letting Brett Farraday have this effect upon her. He was everything she despised—cold, arrogant, a man completely without mercy. How else could he have neglected his young bride, made her life a torment until she had finally gone mad with loneliness and run away? How else could he deny his own daughter? Yet still some primitive part of her own being was drawn to him with a magnetic force. Her gaze roamed the length of the table to the empty seat opposite, then with a quick movement she flung down her napkin and rose, moving out on to the terrace.

She stood breathing deeply as she stared up into the darkening sky. She should never have come here. She had been warned from the first that Brett Farraday was a dangerous man, but just how dangerous she had not realised until now. And now it was already too late.

CHAPTER
FIVE

THE NIGHT air was surprisingly cool and she shivered, wishing she had thought to wear a shawl. As yet she hadn't had time to become accustomed to the sudden drop in temperature as the full glare of the sun's heat died away and the shadows deepened into velvet darkness. Even the earth took on a different scent and she breathed deeply as she listened to the faint trickle of water into the fountain. She would have liked to stay, to linger until the breeze had cooled the burning of her cheeks, but she knew she must get back to Sophie. She felt strangely uneasy about leaving the child alone.

With a sigh she turned, preparing to go back into the house, then stopped abruptly as Brett Farraday came down the steps towards her. Her heart contracted painfully at the sight of him.

'Miss Tarrant, I was looking for you.'

Unconsciously she tensed, her gaze meeting his. 'Then I am sorry, I was just about to return to Sophie. If you will excuse me.' She moved to slip past him, sweeping up the hem of her gown, but to her dismay, as she did so his hand came down on her arm, preventing her. In spite of herself her voice shook as she frowned up at him. 'Please, let me go.'

His mouth tightened. 'You're being foolish. I told you, it isn't necessary for you to sit with the child all the time. She'll come to no harm. One of the servants is with her.'

'I know it isn't necessary. I wish to sit with her, is that so difficult for you to understand?' she flung hotly, as she tried in vain to release herself from his grip. But to her chagrin it merely tightened.

'The only thing I find difficult to understand is your stubbornness, Miss Tarrant.' With a single movement he turned her face so that the light of the lamps fell full on it. Desperately she tried to turn away, conscious of the ravages left by exhaustion that he must see there, but his hand was under her chin and he was studying her remorselessly.

'Have you eaten?'

Suddenly she felt too weary to argue. She shook her head, fighting the threatening tears. 'No, I'm not hungry.'

'Even you cannot exist without food. I thought I gave orders that you were to eat before you continued this vigil, if continue you must,' he said brusquely, and she felt her hands clench.

'You *ordered* me to eat, certainly. Unfortunately, I can't force food down just to please you.'

His brows narrowed. 'Well that's a pity because I mean to see to it that you do just that and I warn you, I'll not take no for an answer even if I have to stand over you until you do. Of course if you prefer that I use force. . .'

Abigail felt anger and frustration rise in her throat. She didn't doubt for one moment that he would carry out his threat, and he still held her arm firmly within his grasp.

'You're hurting me.'

His fingers released their hold but only fractionally. 'Forgive me, that wasn't my intention. Gopal has set out fresh food, I haven't eaten all day and I'm hungry. I want you to join me.'

'I don't see that my lack of appetite need prevent you from eating.'

'Oh I'm sure it won't.' Just for a second his gaze was full of mockery. 'But I'd enjoy it a whole lot more if I could eat without having to worry that you were starving slowly to death beneath my roof, so why not make it easier and spare me the arguments? It would make my conscience so much easier.'

Her chin thrust upwards as she met his gaze. 'I should hate to be in any way responsible for your conscience, Mr Farraday.'

'You surprise me.' The words held a vague note of warning which sent a shiver down her spine. 'I thought you'd made it your own personal crusade.'

'I don't crusade for lost causes.'

'No more do I,' the response came softly. 'Now, will you go in willingly or must I carry you?'

Abigail's teeth clamped together as he moved threateningly. 'I will go, since you put it so nicely.'

He released her and stood aside with a mocking bow as she swept before him, up the steps and into the house. She stared at the table feeling her stomach revolt at the sight of the food, but he was holding out her chair and she knew she had no choice but to sit. Only when she had done so did he move to his own place.

They sat in silence until the servants had gone. Her gaze went to her plate, she picked up her fork but made no attempt to eat.

'It's very good.'

'I'm sure it is.' Her glance met his resentfully. 'I'm just not hungry.' If she was honest, it was only a half-truth. The tantalising smell of the food rose to fill her nostrils. It was his presence which was so unnerving. There was an intimacy about sharing a table. It made her even more

aware of his nearness. The candle flame flickered and
she looked up to see him studying her from behind the
halo of light. She had to fight the urge to get up and run.
Mechanically she began to eat. Her head ached and
there was a strange heaviness in her limbs. Why didn't he
just let her go, did he enjoy taunting her?

She brushed a hand through her hair and started
violently as his fork dropped with a clatter to his plate.
Her glance jerked upwards. 'I'm sorry, did you speak?'

He flung the napkin away, his mouth taut as he looked
at her. 'I've been speaking for the past five minutes, Miss
Tarrant, and you haven't heard a word I said have you?
Am I really such wretched company?'

'No.' The colour drained from her cheeks. 'No. . . it
isn't that.' Even to her own ears her voice sounded shrill
as she tried to convince herself rather than him.

'Indeed, then tell me.'

Her throat tightened. How could she say that his
presence disturbed her, tangled her emotions in a way it
had no right to do. 'It. . . it is nothing. I was simply
worried about Sophie. I really should go to her,' she
finished lamely, rising to her feet.

He rose too, his features thrown suddenly into relief
so that she was made all too aware of the anger in his
eyes. 'Why? Why keep this self-imposed vigil? After all,
what is my daughter to you?'

She drew in her breath sharply. 'She is sick, isn't that
reason enough?'

'No, I don't think it is.' He said it with a bitterness
which shook her. 'I'm beginning to realise that you
aren't like most other people, are you, Miss Tarrant?'

'I don't know what you mean. I'm quite ordinary,
simply doing my job.'

He laughed tersely. 'Oh yes of course, I forgot, your

job. I suppose I should say your conscientiousness does you credit.'

'Not at all,' her eyes flashed. 'I would rather you didn't say anything at all, except that I am free to go. After all, my conscientiousness would scarcely be necessary if you were prepared to play your proper part. . .'

She broke off as his face whitened and suddenly she was glad of the distance of the table between them for she had the feeling he would have liked to reach out and put his hands about her throat. She didn't know what had made her say it—some reckless desire to reach him, to discover some spark of human emotion in him, but she should have been warned that it would be dangerous.

The silence was long and tense until his voice broke it, harsh and controlled, 'For pity's sake, get out of here. Go if you must. God knows I've no appetite left myself now.'

She willed her feet to move, then froze again as his voice stayed her.

'Just what is it about you that makes me want to. . .' His fists clenched and she trembled. 'Dear God, why did you have to come here? I don't need anyone, least of all you.' His fist slammed against the table with such force that she stumbled backwards, blindly seeking the door and escape. Her hand was shaking as it made contact with the handle and she stared wide-eyed as he moved towards her. In one frenzied movement she wrenched the door open and ran. Her gown impeded her progress but somehow she reached the stairs, gasping for breath. Behind her she heard the door slam, the sound reverberating in the vast silence of the house, then she heard the splintering of glass as if he had flung something in anger.

Her heart was beating so fast as she reached the safety

of Sophie's room that for a moment she leaned back, catching her breath. She didn't know why she had run. It had been fear, not of any physical violence but of something else, something she couldn't explain even to herself.

She caught sight of her face in the mirror and was shocked by what she saw. It was flushed and her eyes were brilliant. She looked like a woman who had come from the arms of her lover. The back of her hand went to her lips suppressing a gasp. It was this she feared, that he would touch her, take her in his arms and discover the secret desires of her heart. She closed her eyes, afraid to see more. He mustn't ever know or guess, not when the only thing he felt in return was contempt.

'The memsahib is not well?'

So taken up had she been with her own confused emotions that Abigail had been unaware of the girl's presence until Gita moved from the shadows. Once again she experienced a sense of admiration, knowing it to be tinged with jealousy as she saw the pale blue sari wound about the slender body, and the long dark hair framing the lovely face. Unconsciously she brushed back the wisps of her own escaping hair and thrust away uncharitable thoughts, forcing a smile to her lips.

'I'm fine.'

'The memsahib is flushed. Perhaps she has a fever?'

Abigail shifted uneasily before the intent gaze. 'It is the heat. I doubt if I shall ever get used to it.' She was glad of the excuse which explained away the flush of her cheeks yet somehow she sensed the girl wasn't deceived. It was almost as if she knew what had taken place, the dark eyes were full of hostility.

'It is always so with the English ladies. Their skins are too pale, too delicate.'

Abigail drew in a breath, biting back the anger which rose involuntarily. 'Yes, I'm sure you're right.'

Both physically and mentally she felt too weary to respond to something she didn't understand. There was no reason for the enmity yet it was there. Or was it? Could it just be that she was imagining the whole thing? There was something about this country, about this house, that seemed to be having the strangest effect upon her.

'The memsahib must take care. There are many dangers for those who are not constantly upon their guard.'

'Your concern is most touching, but I will be careful.' She moved towards the bed, glad of a chance to escape as she looked down at Sophie. Any hopes she might have entertained that there had been an improvement died at once but she asked the question anyway.

'Has there been any change?' Frowning she bent to touch the smooth brow and her eyes widened with alarm. 'The fever feels worse. Why didn't you call me?'

The dark eyes held an unfathomable expression. 'Your presence will change nothing. The crisis will come in its own good time.'

'Crisis? What do you mean?' Abigail exclaimed sharply. 'Surely you don't mean she will become worse.'

The girl shrugged with a nonchalance which made Abigail want to shake her. 'It must be. There is always a turning point when the fever will either break and she will get well or. . .' She broke off and Abigail waited with sickening dread.

'You mean she may die? Is that what you are saying?'

The implacable gaze regarded her steadily. 'It is not in our hands. We shall know by morning. Until then there is nothing to be done but wait.'

Wait. Abigail pressed a hand to her heart as it seemed

to hammer in her breast. 'But it isn't fair, she is so young!'

'Death is never fair.' The retort came sharply. 'But why does the memsahib grieve for a child who is nothing to her?'

The words were almost an accusation and Abigail's glance rose challengingly. 'I don't know what you mean. I would care for any sick child. Wouldn't you do the same?'

The finely-drawn brows rose. 'In India one learns quickly to accept death, especially the death of a girl child.'

Abigail knew that her voice shook, that she was betraying a weakness for which the girl despised her, but she couldn't help it. 'But that is heartless, cruel.'

'Would you show as much concern were it not the sahib's child?'

It was some seconds before the full import of the words hit her and when they did colour suffused her cheeks. 'But that is madness. Of course I would care. What possible difference could it make. . .'

'That is something only the memsahib can answer.' Gita's insolent gaze raked her from head to foot. 'But I tell you, he will not accept this child. No more will he accept you. There is no place for you here. You do not belong, any more than she did.'

Abigail reeled before the onslaught which left her breathless, yet even as she struggled to regain her wits the girl was gone, the delicate hands pressed together in mocking subservience before she glided silently from the room.

Still trembling, Abigail sat on the chair beside the bed. It wasn't true, she told herself. Her concern for Sophie had nothing to do with the fact that she was Brett

Farraday's child, such an idea was ludicrous. But her gaze went to the small face, the dishevelled hair so dark, the thick curling lashes veiling eyes which were so like. . . A sob caught in her throat. It wasn't true, it couldn't be true. She couldn't love Brett Farraday, for in that much at least Gita had been right. There was no place for her here and never could be. Elaina had filled the only place in his heart and, whatever had happened between them, there was nothing but bitterness left.

CHAPTER
SIX

THE HOURS passed with nightmarish slowness as Abigail sat watching and waiting for any sign of change in Sophie's condition. Every sound, every slightest movement sent her springing forward, tense with anxiety, imagining that this was the moment she dreaded. The lamps were still unlit except for one close to the bed, and it cast its light on the uneasily sleeping occupant, emphasising all the more her frail grasp on life.

The chair was hard and unyielding against Abigail's back but she refused to move. Once the door had opened and her heart had leapt foolishly, imagining it was Brett, only to fade as she saw Gopal bearing a tray which he set beside her. She wondered, half stupefied with exhaustion, whether he ever slept.

His voice chided her yet was surprisingly gentle, 'If the memsahib will not rest at least she must take some refreshment. I have brought wine.' He pressed the glass of deep red liquid into her hand and she accepted it reluctantly, too numbed by tiredness and anxiety to feel anything. She sipped it to please him and was surprised to feel it's rich-bodied warmth flow through her veins.

'It is very good.'

He smiled, taking the glass, as she pressed a handkerchief to her cheeks.

'The heat, it seems worse. So hot and still.'

'It is always so before the monsoon. Most of the

memsahibs go up into the hills where it is cooler until it is time to rejoin their husbands.'

But I am not a wife, I have no husband to return to, she thought. Her glance went to Sophie. 'How can her father stay away? Has he no feelings?'

'The sahib does care.'

'Then he has a poor way of showing it. I only hope he can live with his conscience, if he has one—which I doubt.' She hadn't meant to unleash her resentment but it had been forced from her by a sense of hopeless frustration.

A shutter seemed to come down over Gopal's eyes. 'The memsahib judges harshly and without knowledge.'

'I judge by what I see, do you tell me I am wrong?'

His hands rose expressively. 'The memsahib does not see all. He was not always so.'

'I find that hard to believe.' She rose to ease her back and moved restlessly about the room.

'The memsahib should have known him when he first brought his young bride to Mandara. Until then his life had been lonely and we all rejoiced that he had at last found a companion to share it and bring him joy. But it was not to be.'

Abigail ceased her pacing to turn and stare at him. 'What do you mean, it wasn't to be? How can you know that? How can you possibly judge?'

'I knew him well. From the first it was clear the new memsahib had no love for this country or my people, or for Mandara.'

'Perhaps Mandara had no love for her.' The accusation rang sharply but if he was aware of it there was no sign in Gopal's steady gaze.

'This may be true.' His voice was clipped. 'But her coming here was a mistake.'

Abigail drew in a sharp breath. 'You presume to know that?'

'She was not right for the sahib. This I knew but the sahib was bewitched. The memsahib was very young and had much beauty. Her skin was pale as milk, her hair the colour of the moon shining upon sand. Such things blind a man easily to the truth.'

Abigail struggled to still the pounding of her heart. 'Which was?'

'That she despised his chosen way of life. To the sahib's face she called it heathen and savage.'

Abigail licked her dry lips. 'You gave her no time. How could she accept all this when all her life she had been accustomed to something so very different?' She tried to move away from his intent gaze yet somehow it held her.

'For some the magic is never there. For others it takes hold and even if they wish it they can never break free.'

She tried to laugh, her heart beating uncomfortably fast. 'That is nonsense.'

He was watching her closely. 'The memsahib knows I speak the truth.

'No, I don't know what you mean.' She pressed a hand to her head. The room was whirling. She felt faint.

'The memsahib has felt this magic.'

She shook her head, trying to deny it, but though her mouth opened, the words wouldn't come. 'Mandara is like a prison. I know only too well why Elaina could not survive here.'

'Sometimes prisons are of our own making. The things from which we wish to escape are not truly the things we fear. The sahib's lady was like a delicate flower, but flowers fade quickly in the heat of the sun.' His mouth was a taut line. 'She was not a fitting wife for the sahib. It was well she left. His pain at her going was great but it would have been greater still had she stayed.'

'Is that why he drove her away?' Abigail realised she was trembling but could do nothing about it. 'Because she couldn't conform? Perhaps he should have remembered that flowers need love and care, but from the little I know of Mr Farraday he is incapable of any such emotions.' She was aware of a stiffening in the Indian's manner.

'Why does the memsahib imagine he refuses the child? It is because he fears to see in her all that he has lost.'

'He must have loved her very much.' *And he must love her still.* The thought whirled in her brain, refusing to be pushed away. 'You know him well.'

A slight inclination of Gopal's head acknowledged the words. 'Since he was baby. I came to Mandara with my wife who was *ayah*.'

Surprise widened her eyes. 'Your wife? She is here at Mandara?'

'Alas, no. She is dead many years.'

'I am sorry.'

His hand rose. 'It is less painful to me now. She was visiting the village of her family and went down to the river one day when Rhanji struck.'

'Rhanji?'

'He was man-eater, very old and very cunning. Sometimes it happens that a tiger will taste flesh and then his appetite is never satisfied until he has killed and killed again. He carried off many villagers—women and babies—before the hunters finally shot him.'

Abigail felt a violent spasm of nausea run through her and closed her eyes until it had passed. 'How. . . terrible.'

'It is past.'

She stared at him. 'How can you speak so calmly, as if it meant nothing?' She knew she was close to hysteria. 'What happens to men out here, do you forget how to feel?'

'Grief does not bring back those who are lost.'

For the first time she saw compassion in his eyes and was ashamed of her outburst. 'You're right.'

'We learn to accept such things with time.'

'Yes, I suppose you do.' She moved across to the balcony, leaning against it, smelling the heady scent of blossoms. Suddenly her teeth caught at her lips as an overwhelming sense of despair enveloped her. 'Unfortunately I don't have time to learn.' She stared into the velvety darkness, her throat aching with tightness. 'There is so much cruelty here and yet so much beauty. I don't know how I shall leave all this behind. My life will never be the same again.'

'The memsahib does not have to leave,' Gopal's voice came to her softly. 'This house has known unhappiness for too long.'

She turned to look at him. 'I'm afraid my being here would change nothing.'

'But it has already begun. Perhaps the memsahib does not see it but it is so. This house needs a woman's presence.'

'A mistress's presence, Gopal, not mine, not at Mandara. I am nothing more than a servant and even if I wished. . . I have no choice. As soon as Sophie recovers, my job here will be finished and I must go back to England.' Her lips quivered. 'Perhaps it's as well, because the longer I stay the harder it will become to leave.'

She turned away, unwilling to let him see the tears

which filled her eyes, and as if sensing her wishes he silently left.

She returned to her chair and dozed, only to be wakened what seemed only moments later by the sound of Sophie mumbling incoherently. To her horror she realised that the crisis had come at last. The fever had worsened and she stared helplessly as the child threshed wildly.

Scarcely aware of what she did, Abigail ran. She had to find Brett. Her footsteps took her to his door and she beat against it, saw it open and fell, distraught and white-faced, into his arms.

'Please, come quickly!' she begged. 'I don't know what to do. We can't let her die, we can't!' Tears streamed down her face but she was unaware of them, of anything but her desperate need to help Sophie. For an instant his features hardened and she realised with a sense of horror that she was holding his arm, her fingers gripping the fabric of his shirt. Quickly she released her hold. 'I. . . forgive me.'

The coolness of his glance quelled her words, he frowned and held the door open. 'How long is it since the fever worsened?'

Her cheeks coloured guiltily, and she cursed herself for having fallen asleep yet again. 'I. . . I'm not sure. Not long I think. Is it. . . too late?' She saw the nerve twitch in his neck as he strode before her leaving her to follow, stumbling blindly, almost running as his long strides took him to Sophie's room. For one terrible moment as he stood stock still on the threshold she feared he would refuse to go in and her heart lurched sickeningly. Then he moved forward slowly and stood beside the bed, staring down at the child. With a sense of shock she saw the lines of exhaustion etched into his face and heard him murmur bitterly. 'Damn you, Elaina, damn you.' Then, as if remembering her own presence, he jerked himself upwards and said sharply, 'You say she hasn't been like this for long?'

She shook her head, praying she was right, that she hadn't slept through the worst of Sophie's ravings. 'I. . . I fell asleep but I'm sure she hasn't. It was her mumbling which woke me and I came straight to you. I didn't know what to do.'

'There is nothing you or any of us can do. She's reached the crisis.'

Abigail didn't move. She could only stare at him in disbelief. 'But. . . I can't believe it, I won't. There must be something. . .'

He rounded on her, his voice taut and brittle, 'There is nothing. Can't you accept that what I'm saying is the truth?'

'No,' she flung at him, tears stinging her eyes. 'I can't accept it, any more than I believe you can, but you are afraid, so afraid that if you show any trace of emotion, if you allow yourself to feel anything you will be hurt again just as you were hurt by Sophie's mother.'

His eyes glittered dangerously but where once she might have shrunk from his anger now she stood her gound. 'You don't know what you are talking about.'

Her chin rose as she faced him. 'Oh but I do. Yes, it's true. I don't know what Elaina did to you, but whatever it was, is it fair that you should make her child suffer for it? She needs you. You need her if you will only bring yourself to admit it.'

She heard the sharp intake of his breath and waited, her body tensed, but the anger she had expected didn't come. Instead he looked at her, only the strength with which he gripped the edge of the chair betraying some inner agony of despair so great that suddenly she wanted to go to him, ease it away. But his voice drew her up sharply.

'What is it to you, Miss Tarrant? Why must you involve yourself in my life?'

For a moment she stared, incredulous, only grateful that he hadn't witnessed what she was sure must have been in her eyes. 'You are mistaken, I have no wish to become involved in your life. My only concern is for Sophie.' She swallowed hard. 'I have become very fond of her. I want her to be happy.'

'Happy?' His brittle laughter stabbed like a knife. 'And you seriously think that she or anyone could find happiness here at Mandara, in this wilderness?'

'Why not?' Her wide gaze clung to his. 'Has it never occurred to you that it is only a wilderness because you have made it so, because you have chosen to shut everything and everyone out?' A tremor ran through her as she said it and she saw his gaze narrow with contempt.

'No doubt you see it differently.'

She frowned. 'Yes, yes as a matter of fact I do. I think Mandara is a house which needs love and laughter to bring it to life, to make it something other than. . . a shrine.' Her voice faded. She couldn't say any more, to do so would be to betray herself and her love for this house and this man. Mandara had wound its way into her heart and she would never be free of it, or of this man, but he must never know it. She clenched her hands together. 'But then as you say, it is nothing to me. I shall soon be gone from here.'

'I don't doubt you'll welcome the escape.' His voice was clipped, edged with sarcasm and she didn't doubt that what he meant was that he would be glad to see her go.

Brushing a hand through her hair Abigail took a step back. The floor seemed to be unsteady beneath her feet suddenly, the hard lines of his features receded and then came closer. Yes, she would be glad to leave if it meant she could find some peace of mind again. She jumped as his hand came down on her arm. Had she spoken the words aloud? She closed her eyes quickly, opening them again as he spoke. His face was a pale blur, too close, and she thrust out a hand. The room was closing in upon her. She had to get some air. Blindly she thrust him away and turned, only to feel herself falling, down, down into the black pit which opened suddenly at her feet. But miraculously something halted her fall. She felt herself gathered up, heard a voice which somehow bore no relation to the look of concern she saw before her eyes closed again.

'You little fool.'

She felt huge tears tremble against her lashes as her body relaxed against the strong, masculine warmth of him. Fingers brushed lightly against her cheek and a cool hand smoothed back the hair from her face before the blackness descended at last, and she let herself slip gratefully into it.

Several times she woke to a world which seemed strangely unreal, in which it was dark and then light. Figures came and went and voices murmured above her making no sense, or was she just too weary to try and understand? It seemed unimportant, she was in no hurry to come back from this safe place except to escape the dull throbbing in her head.

A cold, damp cloth was placed against her brow. She moved restlessly, her eyes flickering open briefly to stare into Brett Farraday's frowning countenance until her bemused brain told her it was all part of a dream. Even the strong arms which supported her and held water to her lips had no reality, no substance. She slept again, half waking, afraid, only to see the shadowy figure standing by the window. Somehow the presence comforted her so that after a while she slipped into an untroubled sleep. But when she woke again the figure had gone and she was left with a feeling of desolation and a desire to weep.

CHAPTER
SEVEN

ABIGAIL's legs felt ridiculously weak, as if she had been ill for a long time, and her clothes seemed suddenly several sizes too large. It was with a sense of shock that she looked into the mirror and saw the dark shadows beneath her eyes. It was as if she had emerged from a state of limbo, knowing neither what day it was nor what hour. Even her attempts at dressing were hampered by the shaking of her hands but she managed finally to fasten the cumbersome buttons at the neck of her gown, and to brush and coil her hair before making her way unsteadily down to the terrace.

She blinked, the glare of the sun hurting her eyes, then drew up with a start as she saw the figure standing alone. She had expected to find the terrace deserted at this hour of the day and hesitated, on the point of retreating quietly as it seemed Brett was unaware of her presence. But Gopal was behind her, bearing a tray, and his eyes lit with pleasure at the sight of her.

'Ah, it is good to see the memsahib restored to health at last.'

'Thank you,' she smiled her reassurance, 'I am much better.' It was impossible now to retreat for Brett had turned quickly and was studying her through a haze of cigar smoke. Slowly, awkwardly, she went towards him. How much of that nightmare had been reality? How much delirium? Frustratingly, there was no answer in his face and she knew a quick, unreasoned sense of disappointment before it was banished by common sense. Of course there was no answer—because there was none to give. She bent her head to the fragrance of a flower, anything to avoid his steady gaze.

'Coffee?'

'Yes, please.'

He poured two cups, watching as she took her place at the table. 'Should you be out of bed so soon?'

'Why not? I'm not ill, I was just a little over-tired.'

'A little more than that, I think. You were exhausted and probably suffering from too much sun.'

'I assure you I don't make a habit of fainting like that.'

'I'm sure you don't, Miss Tarrant, though it's nothing to be ashamed of.'

She drained her coffee then remembered, 'Sophie! Oh no, I completely forgot. . .' She had half risen from the table.

'Sophie is fine. The crisis is passed. In a couple of days she'll be up and about.'

She released a sigh of relief. 'Oh thank God. I don't know how I could have forgotten.'

'It was perfectly natural under the circumstances, don't you ever give up?' A frown of irritation momentarily marked his features and she stared at him.

'No, I don't think I do, Mr Farraday. Now, if you'll excuse me I must go up and see her.'

He rose quickly, his lips compressed. 'Oh for pity's sake, the child will manage perfectly well without you for a while. Can't you see that I'm trying to say thank you.'

Her pulse quickened and colour suffused her cheeks. 'There is no need to thank me.'

'I think there is.'

'I was only doing my job.' The words seemed to be

wrenched from her as he moved closer. 'And now it is
over I am sure we are both delighted.'

His brows narrowed. 'It may surprise you to know that
I *am* pleased Sophie is better. In spite of what you think,
I'm not entirely inhuman.'

He was watching her closely and she found the scrutiny unnerving. 'I really hadn't given the matter any
thought. As I said, all that matters is that it is over. My
job is finished, I have delivered Sophie to you, she is
going to be completely well, therefore I see no reason
why I need remain at Mandara any longer.' She brushed
a strand of hair from her brow as his jaw tightened.

'What do you mean?'

'Just what I say. I shall leave Mandara as soon as it can
be arranged.'

In the prolonged silence he seemed to tower over her,
his chiselled features taut. There was a cutting edge to
his voice when he spoke, 'And what about the child?'

'The. . . I don't understand. You said yourself she is
going to make a full recovery. Certainly she will no
longer need me.'

'I'm afraid I don't agree with your reasoning, Miss
Tarrant.'

She turned to follow his pacing, seeing the tightening
of the muscles round his mouth. A wave of desire swept
through her. Her legs felt weak as she fought against her
emotions. She wanted him but he was totally unaware of
the mental torture his presence inflicted. She had to get
away, it was the only way to retain her sanity.

Her voice seemed to be caught in her throat, 'It seems
perfectly logical to me.'

'But then I never trust a woman's logic, Miss Tarrant.
You say Sophie doesn't need you.'

'That is perfectly true. She has you now.'

'And just what do you think I have to offer?'

'Surely you don't need me to answer that. You are her father.'

'That doesn't make me some kind of god.' Dark eyes looked directly into hers and suddenly she felt trapped. It was a wild feeling, one she couldn't explain, and her hands tightened.

'I'm sorry, but I feel that my responsibility has ended.'

'Then I see I must disillusion you. I've neither the time nor the inclination to play nursemaid. The child doesn't know me or this country.'

'But she can learn.'

'Yes, of course, and that is why I must insist, the child stays only if you remain with her, at least until some other arrangement can be made.'

Abigail was unable to prevent the gasp of horror which broke from her lips.

'But I can't do that, surely you must see. . .' Her voice was ragged with shock and frustration but he seemed unaware of it.

'As you wish,' he shrugged, 'but understand this, if you leave, Sophie goes with you.'

Her face was white now. Why was he doing this? 'But you can't. . . Oh this is madness. I won't be forced. . .'

'Fine,' his challenge met hers softly but full of warning, 'I'll have your things packed and Sophie's too.'

'You wouldn't.'

'Try me.'

Her mouth opened and closed again. She wasn't deceived by the lazy coolness of his gaze. 'You forget, my obligation is finished. There is no reason why I should care what you do. Lady Flixton charged me to deliver Sophie to you, which I have done, and there my duty ends.' She tried to turn away, to accentuate the finality of her decision but his hand snaked out, catching her wrist, and she gasped as, gently but inexorably, she was drawn closer to him and the ice-blue eyes looked down into hers.

'Does it?'

Her eyes flashed defiance. 'I believe so, Mr Farraday. I must. . . I wish to return to England.'

He laughed softly, mockingly. 'And just what is it that you must go back to? To spending the rest of your life looking after other people's children?' Imperceptibly his grip had tightened. She could feel his breath warm against her cheek as she tried to turn away. 'You're not cut out for it, Miss Tarrant. Fate surely intended quite a different destiny for you.'

'How do you know what fate intended for me? What is it to you how I choose to conduct my life? Let me go.'

But he made no attempt to do so. 'You're a fool, Miss Tarrant, or are you afraid?'

'I don't know what you mean.'

'Oh I think you do. You've never married.'

She choked. 'I told you, there were reasons, my father. . .'

'Or was it that you didn't want to get involved, you were too afraid of your own emotions? You do have emotions?'

She felt as if every nerve in her body was responding to his touch. Her eyes closed and she moaned softly.

'You think other people's children can take the place of your own.'

'No, that isn't true!' She tried to twist away but he held her, his other hand bringing her chin back so that she had to look at him.

'You couldn't leave Sophie here with me and you know it.'

'You're wrong, you're wrong!'

'Oh no, Miss Tarrant, you see you forget I listened to you when you were out of your senses with fever. But then, there's probably quite a lot about that time that you don't remember.'

Words choked her as she stared at him. She licked her lips. 'You. . . were there?'

'Someone had to be.' His brow rose. 'Are you shocked? Poor Miss Tarrant, you needn't be. I assure you it was all perfectly proper.'

Proper. He released her and her hand went to her throat, feeling the nerve fluttering beneath the surface. It fell quickly as she remembered other hands, gentle yet strong, holding her, bathing her fevered limbs, remembered lips against her own. How much was the dream? The question rose to torment her again.

She sagged into a chair. 'You are despicable. Yes, you're right, I wouldn't leave Sophie in the hands of a. . .'

'A savage?' he provided.

She glared. 'I couldn't have found a more apt word myself.'

'Oh I'm sure you could if you tried.' The laughter faded and his eyes darkened. 'I take it you'll be staying?' Her hands clenched together as he didn't even wait for her answer. As in everything, he believed in his own right and, angrily, she knew it was true, she would stay because she had no choice.

'Do you ride?'

Her head jerked up. 'Ride? Yes, why?'

'Then go and change.'

'But I haven't. . . Where. . .?'

His mouth compressed. 'I'll have suitable clothes sent to your room. Since you're going to be staying for a while the least I can do is show you the rest of Mandara. If, that is, you think you'd be interested.'

To her surprise she was interested and even pleased. Anything which told her more about this man and his way of life was of interest.

She rose slowly. 'I don't want to keep you from your work.'

'Don't worry, you won't. I have to go out to one of the seams anyway. You may as well come along. Oh and make sure you wear a hat.'

'I don't have one.'

'Then Gita will bring you one, won't you, Gita?'

With a start Abigail realised the girl was standing beside her. She saw the dark eyes narrow with sudden resentment as they looked at him then darted quickly over herself. She seemed about to speak but her mouth merely tightened as she turned and padded silently away on bare feet.

Abigail watched her go, feeling strangely discomfited. 'I'm afraid she doesn't like me but I can't think why? What have I done?'

He bent to refill his cup and for some reason she sensed that the gesture was forced, as if he wished to avoid her gaze. 'You're imagining it.'

'No, I don't think so.'

He drained his cup and put it down impatiently. 'Then I suggest you simply ignore it. Gita will do as I say. As a matter of fact, it occurs to me that you might need some assistance.' His eyes studied her and for some reason she saw contempt mirrored there. 'English ladies seem to, at least the ones I've had the dubious pleasure of knowing. Gita will look after you.'

'That won't be necessary.' Suddenly she despised the idea of being put into a category with the other women he had known. 'I can manage perfectly well alone, I am accustomed to doing so.'

'I'm sure you are, Miss Tarrant, but out here things are different and I'd hate to run the risk of upsetting your precious morals again.'

Abigail clenched her hands together in a supreme effort to prevent them betraying her anger. In everything it seemed he had to dominate and she knew that to argue would be to fight a losing battle. Instead she turned and fled.

She reached her room and stood breathing hard, trying to recover her composure. Brett Farraday had the power to control her emotions and those of everyone about him and he did it with an arrogance which left her feeling helpless. A figure moved, coming out of the brilliant sunlight into the shadows, and as she looked at Gita she sensed again the hostility which lay behind the dark, sensuous eyes. But for once Abigail felt in no mood either to argue or to accept the challenge which seemed to emanate from the girl.

Her glance went to the bed where the promised riding habit was laid out ready. Her hand brushed against the brown fabric, the softness of the high-collared silk shirt and her breath caught in her throat.

'Where did these clothes come from?'

'They belonged to the other English memsahib.'

'The other. . .' Abigail's hand froze.

'There are many of her things. He keeps them all. No one is permitted to touch them, not even I, until now.' The words were hostile and Abigail was struck by the phrase 'not even I'.

'How well did you know her?'

'I did not like her.' The voice was cold and scornful.

'But why?'

'She did not love him.' Anger blazed across the lovely features. 'She was cold, like ice, like all British women.' Gita tossed her head defiantly. 'They know nothing of how to please a man like Farraday.'

Abigail fought the wave of revulsion. 'But you do?'

'Oh yes,' the insolent mouth curved with laughter, 'Gita knows.'

Abigail turned away quickly but not before she was certain the girl had seen and enjoyed her reaction. It had been impossible to hide it as realisation hit her. This girl was admitting that she was Brett Farraday's mistress. Even without words she should have known it, seen it in the look of triumph the girl had flung in her direction. But she hadn't wanted to see, she didn't want to believe.

She was trembling but somehow managed to force herself to appear calm.

'I can dress without your help. You may go now.' Her hands clenched as the girl bowed her head, pressing her long hands together before leaving.

When she had gone Abigail sat on the bed feeling as if the breath had been driven out of her lungs. How could she have been such a fool? How could she have imagined that a man like Brett Farraday would not have a mistress? The bitterness he felt for Elaina was something apart. In a way this was almost a revenge. He was a man with needs—sensuous, handsome, cruel—he would never make the mistake of loving a woman again, but he would use them. Suddenly she felt cold, and there was a faint taste of blood on her lips where her teeth had bitten into the flesh, yet she had felt nothing.

She felt strangely different dressed in the full skirt which emphasised the slimness of her hips, the blouse hugging her neck and the neatly waisted jacket. She stared for a

long time at her reflection in the glass. She was no beauty
but the outfit lent her an attractiveness, almost as if—as
if something of Elaina had somehow enveloped her with
the putting on of these clothes. For one heart-stopping
moment she almost had the feeling that Elaina was in the
room, standing beside her, also approving—or dis-
approving—that reflection.

Abigail shivered violently as if a cold hand had
reached out and touched her and with a sharp cry she
tore the hat with its ribbons from her hair. She would
send word that she had changed her mind and wouldn't
ride after all. But gradually common sense returned.
Brett Farraday could force her to remain at Mandara for
a while but not for ever and in the meantime she would
not remain a virtual prisoner, shutting herself away
rather than seeing him and facing the effect his presence
had upon her. She would not be used. Oh yes, he must
be well aware of the emotions he could arouse within her
and it amused him to taunt her, but she would not give
him that satisfaction. She could school her features if not
her heart.

Warily she made her way downstairs. He was
mounted and waiting, talking to Gopal as she stepped
out into the courtyard. For a moment his gaze rested on
her and she sensed that it was not herself he saw but
Elaina. But his expression betrayed nothing as he said
brusquely, 'For pity's sake, let's go. Another hour and
this heat will be unbearable.'

She allowed herself to be helped into the saddle,
taking comfort in the knowledge that Gopal's eyes at
least offered silent approval. He dismissed the *syce*
sharply as he himself handed her the small riding crop.
'The memsahib need have no fear, this animal is gentle
creature, I chose her myself.'

'Thank you, I appreciate that.' It was a long time since she had ridden and she had no desire to show her fear before Brett. Perhaps somehow the Indian had sensed it.

He stood back then and spoke to Brett who was restraining the impatience of his own mount. She understood nothing of what was said but something in the tone of their voices left her with a vague feeling of unease. It was enhanced when Brett took a gun from Gopal's hands.

Her throat tightened. 'Is that necessary? Are we likely to be in any danger?' She regretted the question as his cool gaze rested on her.

'Only a fool goes out in this kind of country without being prepared, but there's no reason for you to be afraid.'

'I. . . I'm not afraid.'

'No, of course you're not. You're not a very good liar either, Miss Tarrant.'

A denial hung furiously on her lips but the words died. Instead she gathered up the reins and mustering what dignity she could she quickly urged her mount forward, leaving him to follow until he chose to draw alongside, by which time her colour had mercifully faded.

He was right about the heat, she conceded silently as they paused to drink from a leather flask he had brought along. The water was warm and acrid, she grimaced but drank gratefully until his hand snatched it away. .

'Not too much. It's as bad as too little out here. In any case that's all we have.'

'I'm sorry, I didn't realise.' She stifled a feeling of resentment as he took a drink himself and refastened the top, scanning the surrounding area of countryside as he did so.

She followed the direction of his gaze uneasily. 'Is something wrong?'

'Not at all. I was simply checking the lie of the sun, but I suggest we keep moving.'

It was purely instinct which told her he had lied, something in the manner in which he had said it, almost too nonchalantly, but she didn't argue. She nudged her mare forward instead, her own glance warily scanning the scenery now, but there was nothing. Nothing but rocks over which an occasional lizard scrambled in search of shade, and the interminable dust. After a while she decided that it had after all probably been nothing more than her imagination playing tricks. She pressed a hand to her face, brushing back tendrils of hair which clung damply to her cheek. Her back ached but she straightened it unconsciously as he turned in the saddle to look at her.

They rode on. Trees offered a respite from the shimmering glare of the sun but not from the heat which was relentless even as they rode up into wooded hills. But at least there she felt the first faint stirrings of a breeze and her nostrils filled with the heady scent which was so provocative in its beauty and at the same time so elusive. In spite of herself she had to admit there was something about India. Gopal had been right. It seemed to weave a spell, like a thread in a pattern too deep to be unravelled. Its beginnings were imperceptible yet once it took hold there was no escaping. Without being aware of it she sighed and immediately felt Brett's gaze upon her, the dark eyes sardonic, the mouth taut, even cruel.

'I warned you, this is a hard country.'

She shaded her eyes as much from his gaze as from the sun. 'I'm not complaining, Mr Farraday.'

'No, but you will. British women always have some ridiculous hankering after pale complexions.'

She didn't look at him but her chin rose. 'Not all British women. I'm afraid it's a little presumptuous of you to try to slot us all into one category.'

His eyes narrowed momentarily, appraising, then the familiar mockery was there again. 'Perhaps I should have said the ones I've met.'

'Then I'm sorry for you.'

'Goddammit,' his face tightened. 'I don't need your pity.'

Abigail looked at him sharply. 'I'm not so sure of that if your judgment of all females is based upon the experience of one.'

His eyes glinted. 'They don't differ much when it comes to the material things. No man in his right mind would ask a woman to share this kind of life.'

'But why not?' She had spoken before she realised it and saw the sudden furrowing of his brow. Her throat felt suddenly very tight and she had to avoid his gaze.

'Are you a fool or mad, Miss Tarrant, that you need to ask?'

Her hands jerked as the mare bent to nuzzle at some dry grass. 'I don't think I'm either. Perhaps you have been here too long. You see only the bad things.'

'You mean you see something else?' He laughed softly. 'Then tell me.' He was waiting, his expression cynical.

'There is something about India. I . . . I don't know exactly what it is but I felt it from the moment I left the ship, perhaps even before then. Somehow it comes to meet you, an atmosphere, a way of life. . .' She bit her

lip knowing she was blushing but she couldn't prevent it.
She felt awkward, like a schoolgirl, and he made no
attempt to put her at ease. 'I can't put it into words. I
don't expect you to understand what I'm trying to say,
even to me it sounds. . .'

'Naive? Yes, you're right, it does.' His tone was so
scathing that she flinched. 'I can assure you, Miss Tarrant, there is nothing beautiful about disease and poverty.'

'Then why do you stay?' she retaliated furiously.

He shrugged. 'Because it suits me. Because it's better
than the kind of life I'd be expected to lead in England.
Oh, believe me, I've heard all the fancy drawing-room
talk and it's not for me. I can spit further than I'd trust
any politician and my gut turns to see a man being led by
the nose by some female whose one aim in life is to marry
and acquire herself a fortune. That's your kind of life,
Miss Tarrant, not mine. I'm not interested.'

She frowned. 'You have a very strange notion of the
kind of existence I have had, Mr Farraday. It may
surprise you to know that I have never moved in the kind
of circles you speak of. But I don't suppose for one
moment that that will alter your judgment of me or my
kind, as you put it. Not that your opinion is really of any
consequence since I shall not be obliged to endure it for
very much longer anyway.'

Incredibly she heard him laugh.

'I'll give you this much, Miss Tarrant, you've got
spirit.'

'If by that you mean I refuse to be intimidated, then
yes, you are right.' Suddenly she felt angry again as she
realised that, unwittingly, she had revealed more to him
of herself. 'If you have no objection, may we move on.'

'As you wish,' He bowed mockingly in the saddle,

allowing her to go ahead. She did so in silence, stead-
fastly refusing to look back even though she was uncomfortably aware of his gaze boring into her back.

They followed the line of a half-dried river, catching
glimpses of the water between the trees as they rode.
After a while he halted her, his hand on her reins,
silencing her as he pointed. As her gaze followed she
gasped with undisguised pleasure as an elephant lum-
bered into view, thrashing at the water and stirring up
clouds of dust. Fascinated she watched.

'Isn't he marvellous?'

'And dangerous too. He's probably the leader of the
herd, the rest will be close by. The water is low and if the
rains don't come soon he won't find any water at that or
any other hole, and it won't only be the animals that
suffer.'

The thought depressed her as they rode on again,
slowly wending their way through the trees and it was
some seconds before her eyes caught and focused upon
the mass of figures who seemed to be moving like ants at
different levels on the hillside. It wasn't until they had
moved closer that she saw that they were in fact men
working on terraces cut out of the dry rock and earth,
that each layer was gradually being cut away and washed
by a steady stream of water which had been chanelled
towards the workings.

Her eyes widened. 'What is it? What are they doing?'

'Mining rubies.'

She gasped. 'But there isn't a mine. I imagined there
would be shafts—excavations down into the earth.'

He helped her down from her horse, his hands span-
ning her waist with ease, then led her along one of the
terraces. 'It's what a lot of people expect and it works for
diamonds but not here.' The ground was uneven and as

she stumbled his hand shot out to support her, guiding
her amongst the workers—some of them women she
noticed—who were bent, scratching at the earth with
hands or small metal tools. 'Rubies, emeralds and sapphires are found near the surface. That's why we get the
terraces. The workers progress slowly along one seam,
digging and washing out the stones, gradually moving on
to a new layer.' He paused to speak to one of the
workers, took a leather bag from him and tipped the
contents into the palm of his hand. 'These are rubies.'

She gasped involuntarily, 'But they are different,
some are deep red and others are quite pale.'

He laughed. 'Like most people, Miss Tarrant, you
imagine all rubies are red, all emeralds are green and all
sapphires are blue but it isn't so. Sapphires for instance
can be pink or without colour at all, the rarest is orange.
Rubies can be blue, green or even yellow. Here take
these.'

'I had no idea.' She stared with fascination as he took
one of the stones and held it up to the light.

'It needs polishing to gain its fire, then you'll see it as it
should be seen. Unfortunately,' his mouth twisted,
'you'll also see its flaws. Rubies, like emeralds, are soft,
which is why diamonds are valued more highly and
presumably why women prefer them. Their tastes are
remarkably shallow.' She felt his gaze on her. 'What
about you, Miss Tarrant, which stone would you
choose?'

She laughed ruefully. 'Since I am scarcely likely to
own anything of such value it can hardly matter.'

'You should choose rubies,' he said, as if he hadn't
heard her. 'They too have hidden fires.'

She caught her breath sharply, aware of his closeness.
'And flaws too?' she reminded him.

'Not always, and a perfect ruby is beyond price. Unfortunately they are rare.'

She turned away quickly, refusing to read anything into his words, and was glad when he moved away too, giving her time to recover her composure. After a few moments she followed.

He had made his way along the terrace and was calling to one of the men close by. As she watched, the small be-turbanned figure dressed in white approached warily. She heard some words exchanged and was suddenly aware that Brett's voice had risen angrily.

'What is it?' She stood beside him.

He spoke again to the man who responded sullenly before scuttling away.

'My overseer has apparently disappeared.'

'Is that important?'

He frowned. 'Maybe not but I suspect it might be. I've had my eye on him for some time. I don't trust him and he knows it. I also have a pretty good notion of where he is.'

'What do you mean?' She saw the grim expression darken his face and a new feeling of alarm gripped her as, almost impatiently, he took her arm, urging her forward.

She was so intent on finding precarious footholds that it was some moments before she realised that they were being watched. It was the silence which made her first aware of it and she looked up, shocked by the sullenness, the almost wary hostility in the faces of the workers as they stared. Brett's hand moved imperceptibly to his gun and the heads were lowered again but Abigail found herself trembling as she came to a halt.

'Something is wrong, I can feel it. Why are they looking at us like that?'

They had reached the horses and without answering he lifted her into the saddle and mounted his own horse.

'I've been expecting trouble. Someone has been stirring up the workers these past few months. It's all just a little closer than I'd imagined.'

'But what kind of trouble?' Her hands tightened on the reins as she looked at him.

'The men are gradually leaving. At first it was just the occasional one, but that's usual, the sort of thing you take for granted. Some men earn enough to keep them going for a week or so then they take off. But it's more than that now. This is a deliberate campaign to put me out of business.'

'Oh but surely not. Can anyone do that?'

'Quite easily. It's only a matter of time. In this past month four more haven't turned up for work.'

'But why?'

'It's quite simple, because they are scared out of their wits.' His mouth was a taut line. 'And I can't blame them. One of my best workers was killed recently. He was bitten by a snake, there was nothing we could do. Believe me, snakes aren't the problem you might imagine, which makes it all the more strange. As a rule they leave you alone, they only attack if provoked and this man was no fool. We had no choice but to put it down as an accident. It was what happened later that made me wonder.' His fist clenched. 'There was another "accident". This time part of the workings gave way. Another of my best workers fell and hit his head. It was a chance in a million but now the rest of the men are restless. They are beginning to say the rubies are to blame, that they have some kind of evil force attached to them.'

'But that is ridiculous. It isn't possible.' Abigail heard the brittle sound of her own laughter.

'Of course it's ridiculous, to you and me maybe, but these people are superstitious—especially when someone builds on their fears as I suspect someone is doing. They call the stones "Devil's Fire".' He glanced back. 'You've seen for yourself how reluctant they are even to handle them.'

'Devil's Fire.' Abigail's voice faltered as she stared into his rugged profile, the dark hair, the mouth so firmly set, and suddenly there was an irony about the words. 'I'm sorry. But why do the rest stay if they really believe the stones are cursed?'

'Because I pay well. It puts food in their bellies and the bellies of their families, but sooner or later. . .' She saw the knuckles whiten on his hands.

'Is there nothing you can do? Do you know who is responsible?'

'Oh I think I know, and I don't aim to give in so easily.'

She was aware of a sudden new restriction in her throat. 'But surely it won't simply end when your workers are driven away. You can find more.'

'You're right. It won't end.'

'Then what will you do?'

He stared into the distance. 'I may have no choice.'

She was horrified to see his hand stray to the gun and her face whitened. 'Surely it won't come to that?'

His eyes narrowed. 'If I'm given no alternative, yes, I'll use it. I'm afraid I don't believe in curses, Miss Tarrant, any more than you do. What has happened here isn't the result of something supernatural, there is an explanation. Someone wants me out.' He looked at her. 'Do you think I'm going to sit back and let it happen?'

'No,' she whispered. She turned her head away, afraid he might see the fear in her eyes.

'What's the matter? Have I offended your precious morals yet again, Miss Tarrant?'

She blinked. 'Not at all Mr Farraday, nor do I deceive myself that you would care for one moment even if it were otherwise.' And without waiting for his response she dug her heels into the mare's flanks and went on ahead.

It was some time before she realised they had taken a different route back to Mandara. They had crested a hill following a path through some trees when, to her delight, she saw the low roof of a bungalow in the distance. She drew to a halt, excitement at the thought of coming upon some other human being lighting her eyes. 'Look, do you know who lives there? Just look at the way the gardens are set out, why it might be anywhere in England. I can scarcely believe it. Oh couldn't we pay them a visit, please?' She turned in the saddle and bit back a cry as she saw the expression on his face. It was drawn with anger.

'No.'

She recoiled at the violence in his tone. For some seconds she couldn't believe she had understood.

'But why? What is wrong?'

'Nothing is wrong. I have simply said no.'

Resentment flared. 'But you have no right.'

'I have every right.'

Her mouth was dry as her glance went again to the distant bungalow. Was she being unreasonable or was he? 'Is it socially unacceptable to pay calls uninvited, is that it?' she probed.

His eyes glinted and incredibly she even saw him lean forward to snatch at the reins of her mare as if he was afraid she might take matters into her own hands. 'I assure you, Miss Tarrant, social niceties have nothing to do with it.'

'Then what has?' she broke in indignantly. Really, how dare he? 'I'm afraid you will need to explain because I am *not* a prisoner, Mr Farraday. If I wish to visit a neighbour surely I may do so without having to obtain your permission, or do you imagine you can prevent me?' She was breathing hard, trembling, and he nodded grimly.

'In this instance, yes I do. This is the border of my land and you don't cross it without permission, is that perfectly clear?'

Her fingers clenched about the riding crop and she longed to strike him with it. 'You are being unreasonable.'

'Then surely you know by now that I am behaving perfectly in character and that I mean exactly what I say, Miss Tarrant?'

The warning was clear and she bristled with indignation, then some vague memory intruded and her brow furrowed. 'But surely, if this is the boundary of your land, that bungalow must belong to James Peters?'

There was a long silence and Abigail found her hands were shaking.

'What do you know about Peters?'

'Why. . . nothing, that is very little. I met him on the ship coming over from England. As a matter of fact,' her chin rose, 'without his assistance Sophie and I might never have reached Mandara. I have every reason to be grateful to him and I should very much like the opportunity to thank him.'

'Save your breath.' He saw her lips part in a soft gasp. 'Oh I don't doubt you would be well received, too well, but I warn you, keep away.'

Disbelief made the pulse race in her throat. 'I don't think you have any such authority.'

'If you want to challenge it then go ahead,' he drawled coolly, but there was a look in his eyes which made her hold back from putting the warning to the test.

'How dare you? Simply because you have some. . . ridiculous dispute with James Peters is no reason why I should be prevented from the mere politeness of offering my thanks. You are being quite unreasonable.'

'You don't know my reasons.'

'Then I am perfectly willing to listen.' Her eyes blazed with angry tears but if he was aware of them he was unmoved and his mouth tightened.

'Don't push me too far, Miss Tarrant.'

'You mean I am to obey your commands?'

'If you are wise you will do so. Certainly I shouldn't like to have to enforce them by more positive means.'

Her teeth bit into her lips as she tried to restrain the anger within her. 'You don't frighten me, Mr Farraday, I don't care what you do to me but have you given any thought to Sophie?'

His brow rose. 'I hardly see the connection.'

'Then perhaps you should. I suppose it is none of my concern but she is young, surely you can see that she needs friends.'

'You're right, it isn't any of your concern.' He stared at her and she could feel the blood pound erratically through her veins. 'But since you ask, I'll make it plain here and now. I didn't ask for Sophie but since she's here she'll have to learn to be content with what she has. Mandara will be hers someday. Either she will learn to love it or hate it, but either way she'll do it alone, without any help from someone like Peters.'

Confusion and helplessness robbed Abigail momentarily of her anger. 'Are you truly so utterly without feelings that you can condemn a child to such a life?'

His sidelong glance seemed to rake her from head to toe. 'I seem to remember you questioned my ability to feel anything once before, Miss Tarrant. Have I left you in any doubt or must I convince you yet again?'

She drew back sharply, colour burning in her face. Tension held her rigid in the saddle otherwise she was certain she would have fallen. She could see the muscular hardness of his thighs, the tanned strength of his hands and the memory of that other encounter returned all too vividly to confuse and shock her. He had been amusing himself then as he was doing now and she hated him for it.

'You are despicable, Mr Farraday. You don't need to convince me of anything, I have no doubts at all about the kind of man you are.' She flicked the crop against the mare's flanks, galloping away from his gaze and the soft laughter which seemed to follow her all the way back to Mandara.

CHAPTER
EIGHT

ABIGAIL slipped lethargically out of the narrow-waisted jacket and flung off the hat which seemed to be pressing like a heavy weight on her brow. Everything was covered with dust, it was even in her hair. Looking in the mirror she grimaced as she set about removing the pins which had confined it, sighing as it fell free about her shoulders. She was in the act of brushing it with long, energetic strokes when the door opened and Gita came in, carrying a tray which she set on a small table.

'The memsahib enjoyed her ride?'

Without turning Abigail stared in the glass at the figure beyond her own. The feeling of jealousy which rose inexplicably to haunt her was irrational, yet it was there.

'Very much.' Her fingers probed the ache in her brow. 'If only it wasn't so hot.' Putting down the brush she rose, stretching her aching limbs. 'I'd like to take a bath, to lie and soak for hours until the dust is all washed away.'

'I will arrange it if the memsahib wishes.'

'You can?' Abigail turned and saw the girl smile.

'But of course. Come, I will show you.'

Abigail shrugged herself quickly into a robe and hurried to follow. Gita led her along the balcony finally pushing open a door before she stepped aside. Abigail couldn't suppress her gasp of surprise and delight as she stepped into a room tiled with marble, in the midst of which stood a hip bath, ornately decorated with flowers. 'But it's beautiful!' She was ashamed of her ignorance about this country and its people. She had seen men, women and children bathing in the river but had timidly resorted to making best use of the large pitchers of water which were brought to her room for her own use.

'I will have the *abdar* bring water.' Gita indicated glass jars and bottles. 'You will find perfumed oils if you wish them.' Bowing she withdrew, leaving Abigail to wallow in the unbelievable luxury of delicately perfumed water, allowing it to soothe away the aches and tensions from her body. She closed her eyes, letting the water trickle over her skin, only reluctantly finally stepping out, her toes curling against the cold marble of the floor as she reached for the towel and enveloped her body in it. Her hair was damp where she had pinned it against the nape of her neck. She released it, smelling the delicate fragrance of lemon and other scents too elusive to identify.

Her skin was already dry and she reached for her robe. It was as she did so that she caught the faintest movement out of the corner of her eye. For a moment her heart missed a beat then she laughed. It was nothing, a shadow, a trick of the sunlight pouring in through the high window. Then it came again and this time she froze. She felt sick as blind panic rose. A snake began to slither across the floor towards her. She opened her mouth to scream but no sound came. It died somewhere in her throat, stifled by terror as she saw the thing move again, this time in the direction of her bare feet. Blindly she reached out for support, knowing she mustn't move, mustn't lose consciousness, but there was nothing. As she fought the waves of blackness which seemed to be gathering and receding she heard her own stifled sobs and Brett's voice saying over and over again. *They rarely attack unless provoked.* But her whole body was trembling violently and she couldn't prevent it even though she knew the movement alone might be sufficient to make it strike.

She bit back another scream, her head thrown back in terror as she felt the strangely dry skin of the snake against her leg. Sweat filmed her brow but she daren't even raise her hand to brush it away, instead, somehow, she forced herself to look down. The snake had slithered over one of her feet and now lay still, poised. She had always hated the very thought of snakes. This one was quite small but it didn't lessen her revulsion. If only she could call out. Where was Gita? Surely someone must hear her—or would the sound alone be enough to send the deadly fangs sinking into her flesh? How long before oblivion followed and then death?

The snake moved and she had to force down the feelings of revulsion and the instinctive desire to curl up her toes. Almost imperceptibly it wound its way across her foot. Her teeth bit into her lip, drawing blood as its curious waving motion took it to the floor where it lay again unmoving before slithering away.

Her breath was released in a sob of relief and terror as she watched. For some seconds she stood stock still, the towel clasped about her body before the scream broke from her lips and went on and on, seeming to come from someone else.

She didn't know how long it was, it seemed an eternity but must have been only seconds, before the door burst open with a crash and she saw Brett standing there. His eyes raked her body and she saw the look of unmasked appreciation before he seemed to take in the stark whiteness of her face and her outstretched hand pointing to the snake. With an oath he cross the floor and his boot came down. She heard the crack, saw him pick up the thing and fling it away, then she felt herself lifted in his arms, she was aware momentarily of her warm, naked body against his as he carried her from the room and to her bed. He put her down. She was shaking so much that she made no attempt to stop him as his hands moved against her legs and ankles.

'Did it actually bite you?' Grim-faced he was bent over her searching for the tell-tale puncture marks on her skin. His fingers were impersonal yet, dazed as she was, she felt herself rouse to his touch, a sensation of warmth like an electric current passing through her. She tried to protest, drawing the sheet over her body, moaning as he thrust it away savagely. 'Tell me if it bit you.'

She covered her face with her hands, her body still shaking convulsively. 'No. I was so afraid. I couldn't move.' She heard the swift release of his breath as he reached up, his hands crushing her shoulders as he jerked her towards him. Incredibly she could feel the beating of his heart.

'You were right to be afraid. You were lucky. If it had bitten you, you would have been pretty close to death by now.'

'Oh don't,' she moaned, softly. 'It was horrible, like a nightmare. But how did it get in there? Where did it come from that I didn't see it before?'

His expression was grim as he released her abruptly and straightened up. 'That's what I'd like to know too. We don't usually get them in the house, not up here.'

She shuddered. 'I swear it wasn't there until. . .' she broke off, her mind registering something, 'until I lifted the towel as I got out of the bath. Gita had brought it for me and it must have slipped to the floor.' She shook her head. 'What does it matter? I don't want to think about it any more. It's gone.'

'You're right, there's no point in making a drama out of it.'

Suddenly she had the feeling that he had lost interest, that he was annoyed by her attack of hysterics when in fact she hadn't actually been harmed at all. She coloured as his gaze raked once again over her naked body before he strode to the door.

'I suggest you dress. Dinner is ready, I'll wait,' he said, tersely.

She mumbled something incoherent but the door had already closed. Afterwards she sat for a long time before eventually finding the strength to dress and go down and face him.

Purposely she took extra care over her appearance, though whether for her own reassurance or because it seemed best to pretend nothing had happened, she wasn't sure. The only thing she knew for certain was that she couldn't remain there in her room for ever.

She chose a gown which had been purchased to wear at her cousin's engagement ball and which, in the event, she had never had the opportunity to wear after all because her father had fallen ill. The gown had simply been packed away in layers of tissue and forgotten until now. She didn't even know what had prompted her to bring it with her to India but as she took it down she knew she had been right to do so.

Her hands were shaking as she fumbled with the layers of satin. Certainly it was no longer the height of fashion and she too had changed. The subdued colours of mourning had become almost a habit, a comfortable barrier behind which she could retreat, her grief unhindered, but as she stared into the glass now her eyes widened. It was like looking at a stranger, at a woman who was not only attractive but even beautiful.

Her hand fluttered to her throat in a vague attempt to cover the bareness of her neck and shoulders. The gown was too daring. Her fingers strayed to the deep wine-coloured velvet of the short, very full sleeves and the neckline. Cream satin traced with delicate patterns moulded to her waist and hips then flowed into the fullness of the skirts and train and was again edged by velvet. The colours seemed to enhance the paleness of her skin and she blinked hard as the light of the candles seemed to add an air of unreality, casting a glow against her hair which she had swept up into loose curls, allowing soft tendrils to fall against her cheeks. The effect was strangely frightening and she drew in a slow breath. Was it only the gown which was responsible or the thought of the man waiting for her downstairs? Of course she couldn't wear it. Her hands were already at the fastenings. Then she stopped. Why shouldn't she wear it? What was she so afraid of, surely not Brett Farraday? Why he was scarcely even likely to notice.

Sophie was sitting up in bed when Abigail slipped into her room before going downstairs. The pallor was already fading from her face as she revelled in the doting care of the *ayah* who was trying to tempt her to drink a little broth.

Sophie's eyes widened with pleasure as she saw Abigail. 'Oh Miss Tarrant, how different you look. Quite beautiful.' Her eyes appraised the gown with a child's honesty and she reached out to touch the fabric. 'You look just like a princess.'

The lines in the *ayah's* face deepened as she pressed her hands together nodding and smiling, speaking rapidly in her own tongue. Sophie laughed. 'She agrees, I know she does. I'm teaching her English and she is teaching me her own language.'

Abigail smiled as she carefully spread the folds of her gown and sat on the bed. 'That's very good. Of course it will take a very long time.'

'Oh yes, but Jenna won't mind,' Sophie beamed, 'she will do anything for me.'

Abigail smiled but trod warily, 'Then you don't think it will be so bad, living in India after all?'

'I think I shall quite like it.' Sophie tilted her head on one side, considering the matter seriously. 'But I should like it even more if my father wanted me to stay.'

'Oh but I'm sure he does. It's just that you must give him time to get used to it too, you know. After all, it isn't any easier for him to discover that he has a daughter than it is for you to find your father, but it will be fun getting to know one another.'

'He says I can have a pony of my very own.' The large eyes sparkled with anticipation. 'And I'm going to learn to ride as soon as I'm well enough to get up.'

'That's marvellous.'

'Yes, isn't it, and you must come and see me ride.'

Abigail bent quickly to kiss the flushed cheek before rising to her feet. The action served to hide the tears which welled up unbidden in her own eyes as she listened, sensing the child's excitement. Everything was going to be all right, some instinct told her, and she should be happy. She was happy, yet for some reason she was filled with depression, a kind of numbness that encased her heart, at the thought that she would never actually be there to share in Sophie's future, to see her ride, grow up, getting to know and love her father.

She straightened up, moving to the door. 'I shall look

forward to that my dear. Goodnight now, I'll see you in the morning.'

Brett held out a glass to her as she made her way on to the terrace and as she took it she saw the momentary flicker of surprise in his eyes as he raised his own glass to his lips.

'I'm pleased to see you're quite recovered from your ordeal.'

Her hand shook as she sipped at her wine. 'I realise now that it was foolish of me to become so hysterical over something so trivial. I'm quite sure the snake was harmless, it's just that back in England one isn't accustomed to finding them underfoot.'

'On the contrary, I meant what I said, if that particular snake had bitten you, you wouldn't have stood a chance. It was deadly. You had a lucky escape.'

It was only when he took the glass from her rigid fingers and refilled it that she realised she was shaking. She laughed uneasily. 'I'm sorry, I suppose it's delayed reaction.

'There's no need to apologise. Come and eat,' he said, brusquely. She obeyed blindly, scarcely aware of what she ate, though it was good. There was fish cooked in yoghurt and flavoured with almonds and cinnamon, duckling cooked slowly with raisins and carrots and again spices, coriander and garlic, and she caught a faint sweetness of rosewater. Her glass was filled again. She drank automatically and toyed with a sweet of milk and honey and saffron.

With a start she realised Brett was speaking.

'I still don't understand how it got in. That particular species tends to avoid contact.'

She put her spoon down, her throat still too tight to eat

properly. 'I was more concerned with what to do than with how it got there. Then I remembered you said snakes rarely attack unless provoked, though I don't think I was capable of movement anyway.'

'It's as well,' his face hardened, 'But next time you decide to take a bath I suggest you inform one of the servants so that a check can be made, or tell Gita.'

She set her glass down too sharply and pushed her chair back. 'I'm sorry, the air seems very heavy tonight, oppressive almost.' She pressed a handkerchief to her face and stared down at the terrace. He followed.

'It's always this way before the monsoon breaks, that's why most of the women go up into the hills, to Simla or one of the other hill stations.'

Abigail leaned against the low wall, fanning her cheeks. 'When does it come?'

'Around July. Then after the winds we get the rain, if we're lucky, and believe me if you think it's going to be anything like the rain you get back in England you'll be in for a shock. Out here it means the difference between life and death for a lot of people. If it doesn't come there will be another year of drought and if there's a drought there will be no crops and that means trouble.'

Startled she turned to face him. 'Trouble? You mean people will actually starve?'

'People, children—the children first, they haven't the strength to fight the hunger.'

'But that's awful.' She turned away quickly. 'How can there be so much beauty and at the same time so much cruelty? Doesn't it make you feel. . . angry, aware of your own helplessness?'

He didn't answer at once but when he did his gaze was curious, almost wary, 'You want me to believe you care, Miss Tarrant?'

'Surely anyone who has seen it, the country, the people, must care.'

He lit a cigar blowing a cloud of smoke into the air. 'I'm afraid you're remarkably naive if you really believe that, Miss Tarrant.' He frowned. 'For God's sake, what is your name or do I have to persist in this farce of calling you Miss Tarrant?'

Her colour rose. 'It is Abigail.'

'Abigail.' He laughed softly. 'Well it's apt. Have you any objection to my using it or must we stand on ceremony?'

'No. . . I don't object.'

'Good, then that's settled. I'm going to have a brandy.'

She declined his offer to join him, following him after a few moments into the house. Crossing to the piano she lifted the lid and ran her fingers lightly over the keys.

'Do you play?' He was watching her and she felt vaguely uneasy.

'A little. It's been some time. Do you mind if I. . .'

'Please yourself.'

For some reason she sensed that he was angry but the thought was banished as she began to delve into her memory for the tunes she had played for her father. She knew she was no expert but she had a competence, a sense of interpretation, which made listening to her a pleasure. She played idly, for her own enjoyment, picking up the threads of one melody after another, so absorbed in the music and the memories it invoked that at first she wasn't aware that Brett had moved closer. His face was grim. She fumbled the notes and stopped, her hands going to rest in her lap.

'Go on.' It was almost an order but she shook her head, the mood was gone. Suddenly she felt clumsy.

'It's a beautiful instrument.'

'Is it?' He was watching her. 'I wouldn't know. Out here you just order what you want from a catalogue and they ship it out from England.'

'Do you play?'

'No.' His mouth twisted and there was some cruelty in the line of it. 'It hasn't been touched for a long time.'

Abigail looked at him. 'You mean your wife?' She held her breath, anticipating his anger at the intrusion, but strangely it didn't come.

'Yes, my wife. A little toy to please her, to while away the hours, except that there were apparently too many hours and she found other ways to fill them.'

She flinched at the bitterness in his tone but his face was like a mask.

'I'm sorry, I shouldn't have. . .'

'No, go on.' It was almost a command and her mouth was dry as she turned to the keys again. She played without even being aware of what she played. He was standing so close that she could almost feel him. The white jacket he wore emphasised his tan, seemed to make her even more aware of his masculinity, set her pulses hammering. Then, suddenly, his fingers touched her neck, her bare shoulders. It was as if her skin was on fire as pain and ecstasy flooded through her. Her hands struck a discordant note, jarring, then froze over the keys, unable to go on. Her eyes closed, then in one wild movement as she tried to move away, to escape, his hands reached out as he caught her, pinioning her arms to her sides and she was forced to look up into his eyes.

'Why did you stop?' His fingers were moving against her cheek, making her feel weak.

'I. . . I have a headache. In any case I play very badly. I'm sure it can't be much pleasure for you.'

He was staring down at her, his mouth taut and she looked away, confused by his expression. 'You're a liar, Abigail Tarrant.'

'No.' She shook her head, the word little more than a whisper but still he held her.

'I'm not entirely a savage you know. I choose to live in the wilderness but that doesn't mean I can't appreciate the finer things. My wife did manage to educate my tastes at least a little.'

Her mouth was dry. His hands seemed to be burning against her flesh. 'I'd really rather not play any more. I am very tired.'

He released her abruptly and she moved from the piano hoping she wouldn't faint. She held on to a chair then raised her head to stare at him, confusion and resentment, so many emotions welling up inside her, turning her blue eyes darker in the whiteness of her face.

'Did you ever love your wife?' she asked it, trembling, and the expression in his eyes made her regret the question.

It was some time before he answered and she saw the steely glitter in his eyes, the tenseness of his hands. 'Yes, I loved Elaina, before she made me realise that I hadn't married a woman but a spoilt child who thought life out here was going to be nothing but a social round, with my catering to her needs, her wishes. She hated India, she hated Mandara, finally I suppose she even hated me.'

'She was young. Did you ever make allowances, give her a chance to learn?'

He laughed softly, his mouth twisting bitterly. 'Elaina didn't want to learn. Oh yes, she was young, but in that she was no different from the hundreds of other wives who come out here. What she couldn't face was that I wouldn't—couldn't dance attendance on her twenty-four hours out of every day, wouldn't escort her to parties. The truth is, she just couldn't live without her rich society friends but I suppose the fault is mine. I should have known it wouldn't work.' His fist clenched against the chair. 'It was like tearing a rose up by its roots and expecting it to live.'

Abigail swallowed hard. 'Perhaps things might have been different. . .'

'How? If I had given up everything, devoted my life to nothing but making Elaina happy?' He swore savagely. 'Perhaps I expected too much. I had no right to ask any woman to share the kind of life I lead.'

'But that isn't true.' She broke in without thinking. 'You can't spend the rest of your life allowing the memory of Elaina to make you bitter. It was a mistake. Perhaps for Elaina it would never have worked.'

'You know about such things do you?'

Her colour rose at the scorn in his eyes. 'Gopal once said India has a special kind of magic, some never know it, others are aware of it from the moment they set foot on its soil. I know what he means. I felt it.' Her voice shook but she forced herself to go on. 'I shall always feel it, even when I have left Mandara. I think. . . it will haunt me.' Her hands tightened and she felt the nails bite into her palms. 'You can't, you mustn't judge all women by Elaina.'

He was silent for so long that she was afraid she had said too much. She had turned away and so missed the expression on his face. When she looked at him again, afraid that he had walked away and left her, he was staring at her so intently that she experienced a sense of shock. He flicked away the cigar he had been holding.

'You don't have to leave.' The liquid dark eyes scanned her face and she couldn't speak. 'You said yourself you've nothing to return to, so why go? Why not stay?'

Her hand rose to her throat as she stared at him, uncomprehending. 'I. . . It's quite impossible.'

'Why?' His eyes narrowed.

'B. . . because. . .'

'Because you're afraid, that's it, isn't it?'

She tried to laugh. 'That's ridiculous. Why should I be afraid?'

'Ah.' He took a step towards her. 'That, Miss Tarrant, is something only you can answer.'

'I thought I had already done so. There is no reason for me to prolong my stay. You know that, we both know it. Sophie is almost fully recovered. She won't need me. I couldn't,' she was stammering, 'I couldn't stay, it wouldn't be proper.'

'Proper.' She heard the sharp intake of his breath and then his laughter. 'My God, you're priceless.'

She froze, her heart pounding wildly as he moved yet closer.

'What the devil do you think I'm proposing?' He stared into the shocked depths of her eyes. 'Dammit woman, don't look at me as if I'd just tried to rape you. I'm not asking you to be my mistress, I'm asking you to be my wife, or does that offend your precious virtue too?'

CHAPTER
NINE

ABIGAIL knew that the colour had drained from her face leaving it white. A pulse hammered so violently in her throat that she was sure he must see it. Of course she had mistaken his words, that must be it. They had been spoken so utterly without emotion. Even now as he stared down at her, the dark eyes boring into her own, she looked for some sign that it was possible he had spoken them and found none.

'Marry you?' The combined strength of her own emotions and his nearness were doing strange things to her.

'Well?' He frowned impatiently and poured another glass of wine, holding it out to her. 'Here, you'd better drink this.'

She obeyed mechanically. She had already drunk more than was her custom and it had made her quite pleasantly light-headed, yet now the sensation vanished, leaving her coldly aware of all that was happening.

'I must say I don't find your reaction to my proposal very flattering, Miss Tarrant.'

She blinked, trying to brush away the feeling of incredulity. 'I'm sorry. It's just that I wasn't sure. . . You did ask me to marry you?'

'Obviously the idea repels you.' He was studying her calmly, too calmly, she thought.

Her head jerked up. 'No, it doesn't repel me, Mr Farraday. What does offend me is that you can make a

joke of something so serious. I find your sense of
humour both strange and distasteful.' She put down the
glass and tried to walk past him pretending that her heart
wasn't rent in two by the savage knife-thrust of his
cruelty, but the tears stung beneath her lashes and she
gasped involuntarily as his hand came out, closing over
her arm in a steely grip. Her gaze flew up to meet his,
angry protestations on her lips, but they died as she saw
the grim anger in his face.

'Do you seriously imagine I'd joke about such a
thing?'

She flinched at the ice in his tone. He seemed unaware
of the pressure he was exerting on her arm or the pain it
caused, but she couldn't free herself.

'Then why?' she demanded, furious with herself for
the threatening tears. 'I don't understand. How can you
be so cold-blooded?'

His mouth twisted cynically. 'What do you want,
protestations of love?' His hand moved, raising her face
so that she had to look up at him. 'If that's what you
want. . .' His eyes mocked her and she turned her head
involuntarily, colour flaming in her cheeks.

'You are despicable. The last man on earth I would
wish to marry.'

He released her and she was glad, glad because at any
moment he might have seen the truth in her eyes.
Instead his brows drew together. 'I'm not insisting that
your emotions have to be involved, Miss Tarrant. I've
asked you to marry me but I assure you you needn't fear
that I would press my attentions upon you, knowing how
unwelcome they would be.' His gaze was dark, like
glittering black stone, 'What I'm suggesting is purely a
marriage of convenience. I thought you would realise
that.'

The blood seemed to freeze in her veins. 'A marriage of convenience?'

'Of course. What else?'

Yes indeed, what else? The thought hammered in her brain, mocking her.

'I'm thinking of Sophie, as you have so often urged me to do. You care for her and I, it seems, am cast in the role of parent whether I choose or not.' He bent his head to light another cigar, shading the flame with his hand as he stared at her through the thin haze of smoke. His eyes held reflections of the brilliance but the rest of his features were shadowed like a mask, concealing his innermost thoughts. 'What's the matter? I thought you'd be pleased. Or is it that you still mistrust my motives, my . . . husbandly intentions? I promise you, you will be free to do as you please, within certain inevitable bounds of course. I shall expect you, at least outwardly, to appear in public whenever necessary as my wife. It goes without saying you'll be responsible for Sophie. She needs a woman's guidance, I realise you were right about that, and of course you will be mistress of Mandara.'

Her face was white as she looked at him. 'It would be quite impossible of course, you must realise that. I couldn't agree to something that would be nothing more than a. . . a farce.'

'I don't see any such thing. It may seem a farce to you but if you take my name you also take on the responsibilities. Of course I regret there must be some strings if it is to look right. The servants will expect it.'

She shivered. He seemed to be taking over her life. She would be his wife, *his wife*. In silence she said it over and over again until she had to press her hands to her head to still the pounding. But it meant nothing. As far as he was concerned it would be a loveless marriage. He needed a mother for Sophie, someone to ease his own conscience, nothing more, and she had been fool enough to let him see that she cared. Oh yes, he had offered her his name, a position as mistress of his house, but not his love. That was to play no part in the bargain. A vision of Gita drifted into her mind, taunting, smiling. She closed her eyes, feeling as if a hand was clamped about her heart. She knew he was waiting for her answer but she couldn't speak. Instead she paced away from him, her hands clenched. How could she stay here, each day bearing the bitter irony of loving him, of knowing she was his wife yet knowing that her love would never be returned?

'Is it really such a difficult decision to make, Miss Tarrant?' His voice followed her relentlessly, drawing her to give an answer and she turned to face him. She had only to say no.

'I. . . I will accept your proposal, for Sophie's sake, because I would rather not contemplate the kind of life she would be condemned to live otherwise.'

For the merest fraction of a second she thought she saw relief flicker in his eyes. And why not, she thought bitterly, after all he had merely played upon his knowledge of her affection for the little girl. In reality he had given her no choice at all. But was that the real reason, some small voice whispered in her ear and was thrust away.

His features were impassive as he crushed out the cigar and studied her.

'You won't regret it.'

She wanted to say that it was already too late, that she regretted it even now, but she stood immobile, mustering all her self control as he moved closer.

'I can only hope you are right.' She tried to match his own calmness, his indifference, feeling it drive a wedge into her heart.

He was looking down at her, his hand on her arm. She was shaking and he was aware of it. 'You are sure?'

She hesitated. There was still time to draw back. She nodded. 'Perfectly sure, Mr Farraday. You needn't be afraid I shall change my mind. I love Sophie but then, you already know that.'

For an instant his eyes narrowed. 'I just want to be certain you understand.'

Every nerve in her body screamed to be allowed to escape. Oh yes she understood, only too well, that she would not be permitted to interfere in his life. 'Don't worry, I have no intention of going back on my word, in any respect whatsoever.' Why oh why didn't he just go away, leave her alone to give vent to the tears which were welling up like a torrent inside her. Suddenly his nearness provoked her to anger. 'I shall fulfil my part of the bargain just as I expect you to fulfil yours. In public I shall behave as you would wish a dutiful wife to behave.' Her lips trembled. 'As for caring for Sophie, that will be easy and a pleasure. But for the rest. . . we shall both be perfectly free to lead our separate lives. Have I understood you correctly?'

Without answering he crossed to the table where he poured two glasses of brandy and offered her one. She had never drunk so much in her life before but now she was glad of the strong spirit which burned through her like a fire, yet somehow failed to melt the lump of ice which was her heart.

'Let's drink a toast, to our. . . arrangement.' He raised his glass and with a supreme effort she managed to respond. He was inhuman, she thought. 'I'll make the necessary arrangements,' he was saying. 'I don't see any point in delaying, we may as well make it for next week.'

Her eyes widened. 'So soon?'

'Have you any objection?'

No, she hadn't. None she could voice. She shook her head.

'Good. As far as Sophie is concerned I think the sooner the better, not that I think she will find it difficult to adapt to the idea of you as her mother. She is already fond of you.'

It was all like a nightmare. Silence hung between them as Abigail tried to adjust mentally to the idea that she would indeed be Sophie's mother. It was the one part of the whole bargain which gave her a sense of happiness, which would make the rest more bearable.

'As you say, the sooner Sophie adjusts to the situation the better.' She looked at him, her pride searching for some chink in his armour, some sign of emotion, but the hope was dashed. 'Will you tell her?'

'Don't you think we both should?'

Her hand rose. 'Don't you think she may find it a little. . . strange. I mean, I know she is only a child but surely she must realise that we. . . I. . .' She broke off helplessly and he finished it for her, his eyes never leaving her face.

'That we aren't in love, you mean?'

Once again she was aware of the mockery in his tone. 'I suppose I do.'

'Children take things at face value, Miss Tarrant. They don't look for subtleties. They accept what they see and if necessary it can be arranged.'

She frowned. 'I don't understand. Arranged? How?'

'Really, you are naive.' Suddenly he was looking down at her. She felt the constriction in her throat, the drum-beat of her heart, then his hand touched her neck, his fingers cool against her burning flesh, the other was at her waist drawing her inexorably closer.

She couldn't breathe. Her body tensed and she moaned softly but there was no escape. In the light of the lamps she saw his face, tanned and strong and quite without mercy, as for a long moment they gazed into each other's eyes. Then she heard the sharp intake of his breath before his mouth came down on hers.

She tried to resist, this wasn't part of the bargain, yet some primeval instinct deep within her responded and her lips yielded to his. Her fingers rose instinctively to the nape of his neck and his own hands tightened spasmodically, drawing her even closer against the mascular hardness of his body, moving over her hips, back and shoulders. A tide of passion swept through her like a forest fire. She wanted him, to be possessed by him, to feel the pain and the ecstasy of his love-making. Then, as suddenly as it had begun it ended. His hands paused, biting into the naked flesh of her shoulders as he put her from him. Had he released her completely she knew she would have fallen. She felt drained, cheated and confused. What had happened? How could he kiss her like that in one moment and in the next look at her as he was now doing, with studied contempt.

'Oh yes, I think it will be easy enough to convince anyone don't you, Abby, if we put our minds to it?'

She bit back a gasp of shock, feeling as if all her strength had left her. She could only stare at him, her eyes wide and stricken, wondering what on earth had possessed her to agree to such a bargain. For what was the use of agreeing that there should be no ties when those ties were already there, binding her own heart to him for ever?

CHAPTER
TEN

IT WAS done. Abigail was Brett Farraday's wife, yet even though she said it over and over again in the silence of her room, the fact had no more reality now than at any moment of the week which had led up to it.

At least he had been right about Sophie's unquestioning acceptance of their announcement, she thought. They had told her together and she had flung herself with a cry of delight into Abigail's arms crying, 'Oh I'm so glad. You won't have to leave after all and I shall have you to myself for ever and ever.' Then she had looked up shyly. 'You'll really be my mother?'

Abigail had had to swallow hard to remove the lump from her throat as she nodded. She was conscious of Brett watching her and purposely avoided looking at him. 'Yes, I shall really be your mother.' Then Sophie's tears had mingled with her own, the only difference being that the child's were tears of happiness, she thought, as she released Sophie to run and tell her *ayah* the news.

Afterwards, with a new kind of awkwardness between them, Brett had said, 'I suppose under normal circumstances we would settle for Europe or England for a honeymoon, but as the circumstances are scarcely normal I suggest we content ourselves with Darjeeling. Not exactly romantic but then we're not looking for romance are we?' Then, seeing the shock in her eyes he added quickly, 'Unless you have somewhere else in mind, some particular preference?'

She stifled a feeling of panic. 'No, it isn't that. It's just that I hadn't imagined. . . Surely a honeymoon isn't necessary. You said yourself the circumstances are scarcely normal. Can't we just remain at Mandara after we are. . . married?' She saw the frown which touched his strangely cold handsome features.

'No, I'm afraid that won't be possible. It will be expected that we go away and I thought I'd made it clear that I wanted everything to appear normal, even if it isn't.' He saw the sudden colour in her cheeks and mistook it for fear. 'Oh don't worry, you and I will know the truth and I see no reason why we shouldn't try to make the best of the situation since it is forced on us.' He brushed a hand through his hair. 'God knows, the tongues will already be clacking, we may as well give them something to talk about even it if isn't for real.'

'How long shall we be away?' she said, huskily.

'That's up to you. A week, two weeks, a month.'

'No.' She said it too quickly but how could she bear to be alone with him for that long, carrying out a pretence which could be nothing but torture. 'There seems little point in prolonging it, does there, even for appearances' sake, and there is Sophie.'

'Oh yes,' he conceded, in a tone which left her feeling confused. 'There's Sophie.'

She stared at him, wondering what he had expected. After all, wasn't that the very reason for their marriage? Surely he couldn't resent her concern? 'She's very young to be left alone with the servants.'

'They dote on her or hadn't you noticed? I wouldn't have believed that she have wound them all round her little finger in so short a time. You'll have your work cut out when we get back trying to instil some sort of sense of responsibility into her.'

'I think there's time enough. It can't do her any harm just to enjoy herself for a while.'

'As you wish. I leave that sort of decision to you, naturally.' Stung by his sudden apparent boredom with the subject she clenched her hands, glad when the meal was over so that she could escape the close proximity of a shared table. 'I'll make the arrangements. As you say there's no point in prolonging the farce. In any case I'm uneasy about being away from the mine while the men are so restless.'

And so it had been arranged, coldly, without any of the excitement she had always dreamed would attend her wedding day. It might have been a business transaction. 'Which it is,' she thought, dully, as she stared at her reflection in the long, gilt-framed mirror and saw not herself but a woman who was a stranger.

The woman standing there was married. There was a ring on her finger, a wide gold band which sat uneasily. She wore a gown of ivory satin and lace, high-necked, the bodice moulded to her figure, the sleeves full and gathering into a cuff at the wrist, the skirts heavy as they fell into a train behind her. This woman was beautiful.

But all brides are beautiful, the thought had driven the tears at last to her eyes as she took her place and turned to the man who was to be her husband, seeing the expression which flickered in his eyes before his mouth had become a taut line and he had not looked at her again as the simple words of the ceremony bound them inextricably together.

It had passed in a haze of unreality. She knew she must have made the appropriate responses, faltering when her mouth became so dry that she could scarcely speak, knew that he had taken her hand in his and slipped the ring on to her finger, retaining his grasp when he must have seen from the whiteness of her face that she was near to fainting.

And then when it was over, the congratulations from people she didn't know. Somehow she had managed to smile and had sipped at the glass of wine Brett had placed firmly in her hand.

Then, mercifully, he had led her out on to the terrace. She had been dreading the intimacy of the first moments alone with him but his voice was gentle as he took the glass from her nerveless fingers and set it down.

'Won't the guests be wondering where we've got to?' She glanced nervously at the crowded room but he seemed in no hurry to return.

'It won't hurt them to wait and wonder. In any case, why should they? Isn't it usual for the bride and groom to want to be alone?'

Was he being deliberately cruel? She shivered. 'I'm cold.'

His eyes searched her face intently, hard and questioning. 'Are you trying to run away from me?' Then, even as she tried to protest, his finger tilted her chin up so that she had to look at him. 'Poor Abby, was it such an ordeal?'

She swallowed hard. How easily he read her mind, yet he wouldn't allow her to escape. It had to look right for the guests, they were a bride and groom savouring their first few moments alone. 'You look beautiful,' he said, and then, suddenly he had drawn her close and was kissing her in a way that seemed to find every sensitive area of desire within her. She tried to move, to resist, yet his very gentleness was utterly ruthless. He released her as she moaned softly, his touch sending waves of unre-

quited passion flooding through her. She pressed a hand
o her mouth, shivering, her taut resistance returning as
ae frowned.

'I think our bargain entitled me to that at least,' he
aid, brusquely, 'after all, we did agree that in public at
east we would try to behave as man and wife.'

Her head jerked upwards as the shaft seemed deliberately aimed to hurt her. Shock widened her eyes as she
aw the curve of sardonic amusement on his lips and
lowly, very slowly, she drew herself up. So she had been
ight. He had been taunting her. It had all been part of
he bargain.

'I'm sorry if I haven't played my part very well.' She
vas surprised to hear her own voice sounding so calm
vhen inside a tumult raged.

'You look like a ghost. I thought brides were supposed
o have some colour in their cheeks. The flush of anticipation perhaps.' He was mocking her and her hand
vent defensively to her face. It was burning and for a
orief moment his fingers brushed against her skin.
Don't worry, right now you look like a wife who has just
oeen kissed by her husband. It wasn't so distasteful, was
t?'

A response choked her. Why was he doing this when it
vas he who had set the conditions of their bargain,
naking it perfectly clear that he expected nothing from
ner? But in her heart she knew the answer, he was simply
eminding her that he expected her to keep her side of
he bargain. In public they were man and wife. But did
hat mean she must endure his kisses, knowing that in
eality it was all a game.

She closed her eyes briefly, not knowing how she
vould bear it, yet for Sophie's sake she had no choice,
and in any case it was too late now. The ring on her finger

was reminder enough that she was now Mrs Brett Farraday.

'We'll be leaving soon.' His voice roused her from her misery. 'I suggest you go up and change before we say our goodbyes to the guests.'

He had left her then and she had fled blindly up the stairs to her room breathing hard and blinking back the tears to stand before the mirror.

Too late for turning back and there was still the worst part of the ordeal to be endured. Suddenly the thought of being alone with him for two weeks whilst they went through the farce of enjoying a honeymoon filled her with dread.

She had chosen to change into a gown of damasked satin in a shade of blue-green which, she had to admit was quite the most stunning thing she had ever owned. It had been part of Brett's wedding gift to her, despite her protests that it was not necessary to go to such lengths in order to keep up the deception. His response had been cool yet firm.

'I see no reason why you should cling to that semi-mourning. You'll be my wife, mistress of Mandara, choose whatever you like from the catalogue or write down your measurements. Whatever you require will be delivered in time.'

She had obeyed, even finding pleasure in acquiring new things, though she had purposely limited her purchases, and she was pleased with the outfit she wore now. It was worthy of any bride she thought, wryly, as she slipped into the full skirts. A tiny bolero completed the picture, with leg-o-mutton sleeves and blue-green velvet revers. She fingered the gold embroidered bands which decorated the white frills at the neck and wrists then carefully arranged a straw hat with its lace and plume trimming upon her hair, drawing the fine veil over her face. Gathering up her silk gloves and a lace parasol she slowly descended the stairs. It was time to go, the guests were getting restless for their departure.

Brett was waiting for her. His glance rested appreciatively on her for a moment before he led her out to the carriage, seemingly oblivious to the laughter and good wishes which followed them. Abigail's throat was dry and tight as she bent to kiss Sophie who was flushed with excitement and refused to be still despite the flustered pleading of her *ayah*.

'Don't forget to bring me back a present,' she reminded as Abigail allowed herself to be handed into the carriage.

'I won't.' How hard it was to leave her behind. She smiled, glad of the veil which hid her tears. Brett made a last minute check of their luggage. It seemed impossible that they could need so many trunks but somehow room was found for everything.

Gopal's white-coated figure came down the steps towards her and for a moment the enigmatic features met hers. 'The memsahib will not regret,' he said, softly. 'In my country we marry first and wait for love to grow.'

Somehow her frozen lips formed a smile. 'Oh Gopal, what am I to do?'

He shook his head imperceptibly. 'The memsahib need not fear. It is already begun. The sahib believes his heart is dead but the fire is there only waiting to be rekindled.'

She bit her lip. She couldn't bring herself to say that she was not the woman who could ever bring that flame to life again. The memory of Elaina was too strong.

'The memsahib will find the strength.' He bowed and stepped back leaving her no time to reply as Brett climbed into the carriage beside her. Then they were away. She turned to wave until the house and Sophie and Gopal faded at last from view then sat back in her seat, acutely conscious of the man beside her.

It was a long, tiring journey and even though she sat with the parasol shading her from the fiercest heat of the sun, by the time they eventually reached their destination her head was thudding with tension.

It increased as they were shown to their suite where a servant carried up their trunks and salaamed before closing the door and leaving them alone at last.

Brett moved about the room, approving its airiness and the furnishings. Abigail's own feet seemed incapable of movement as her gaze was drawn to the large bed with its hangings and the covers turned neatly down. Her hand went to her throat. Surely he didn't mean that they should share it, yet where else. . .

'I suggest we dine and get an early night. You must be exhausted.'

Wildly she dragged her gaze up to meet his. 'Yes, I am tired.' Her voice sounded strangely unlike her own. She wanted to say she wasn't hungry but she clung to anything which would postpone a confrontation. Automatically she sat before the mirror rearranging her hair, trying to still the feeling of panic. What could she do if he chose to break his part of the bargain? She was his wife. What would she want to do? She glanced up to find him watching her, his expression disturbing, and her heart began to race as she rose quickly and reached for her satin purse.

They dined by candlelight and to the sound of music. The food looked exquisite yet tasted like chaff in her mouth so that she had no idea whether she ate fish or chicken.

'Doesn't the meal please you? Would you prefer something else?'

She jerked her gaze upwards. 'No, thank you, it's delicious. I'm just more tired than I had realised.' She stared at her plate.

'Perhaps you'd rather go to bed.'

'Yes.' Colour stung her cheeks as she thrust away the napkin. 'If you don't mind.'

'Not at all.' He refilled his glass. 'You don't mind if I stay a little longer?'

'Of course not.' She rose to her feet, clumsy with tension. 'I. . . goodnight then.'

He raised his glass in salute, staring at her through the blood-red liquid, his expression betraying nothing as she hurried away.

She undressed quickly, slipping out of her gown and into her coolest nightgown before releasing her hair from its pins and letting it fall loose over her shoulders. For the first time in her life she didn't even brush it the required one hundred times before getting into the bed where she lay huddled beneath the sheets, listening and waiting for the sound of his footsteps outside the door. She closed her eyes, trying to force her limbs to relax but it was impossible. He was her husband, he had every right to come to her if he chose. But he would not choose. A slow, soft anger began to stir in her. She turned over, stifling a sob as she beat her fists into the pillow, and she saw the gold band on her finger. She wanted him, wanted to be possessed by him. She knew now that she couldn't fight him, wouldn't even want to try.

Her tears dampened the pillow and eventually she must have slept for a sudden sound woke her. Her lashes flew open and in half-sleep she couldn't remember where she was. The room was unfamiliar and the covers had slipped from the bed leaving her feeling chilled.

'Who is it? Who's there?' She half rose on her elbow and with a feeling of terror saw that the door was open.

In the pale light cast by the moon he saw the tension in her face as he moved slowly towards her. Memory came flooding back.

'Brett. . .' her voice faltered. 'You startled me.'

'I'm sorry, I didn't mean to alarm you.' She watched as he took off his jacket and moved towards the bed. Instinctively she pressed back against the pillows, every nerve tensed as she watched him.

He came to a halt and stood looking down at her. Colour rose in her cheeks as she fumbled for the sheet in order to cover her semi-nakedness. He frowned at the gesture and the uncertainty in her eyes.

'Why are you afraid of me?'

Afraid? Was she afraid? Not of him, only of the power he seemed to have to throw her emotions into utter turmoil. She stared at him. 'I. . . I'm not afraid. Why should I be?'

'Why indeed?' He stood looking down at her, swaying slightly, and she felt the pulse hammering in her throat. He bent for a moment, his hand brushing against her cheek and she flinched unwittingly, afraid only that he would sense the feelings that his touch could rouse.

His jaw tightened. 'Do you still hate me so much, Abby? Am I so repulsive to you?'

She gasped. 'No, that isn't true.'

'And yet you shrink from my touch.' His hands moved and it was as if a fire spread over her ice-cold flesh.

'Please,' she moaned softly, 'Don't, Brett. We made a bargain.'

'Oh yes, a bargain.' He laughed bitterly and she

smelled the wine on his breath. 'I agreed, didn't I, that we should have a marriage of convenience. I needed a mother for Sophie, but that doesn't mean I don't have desires, Abby, desires which you can fulfil.'

She, or any other woman. She closed her eyes feeling the tears spill between her lashes on to her cheeks. 'You've drunk too much. You don't know what you're saying.'

He was very close, his face only inches from her, his hands forcing her to look at him. Beneath the sheet her heart was hammering.

'You're right, I have had too much to drink. If I hadn't I'd probably walk out of here now and leave you to your virgin bed. That's what you want isn't it? Just like Elaina. She fell in love with a dream and when it didn't match up to her ideal she ran away. But not you, Abby, not you. You'll stay if only for Sophie's sake.'

She recoiled, sobbing. So it was revenge he wanted. She must pay for what Elaina had done to him. He stood up and began removing his clothes, flinging them to the floor. She sat up, throwing the covers back, but it was too late, he caught her and his weight crushed her beneath him. To struggle would have been futile, his strength was so much greater, and yet as his hands moved skilfully over her body she didn't want to escape.

Sweat filmed her skin and she groaned softly, then more wildly as his love-making became more demanding, more ruthless. Pain seared through her and she cried out. The weight moved from her but she lay unmoving, her nightgown torn, tears falling to the pillow where she turned her head away. She heard his muttered oath, felt his hand jerk her face round and his mouth come down painfully on hers before he broke away.

'Forgive me,' his voice rasped.

She couldn't answer. For the rest of the night she lay
awake, staring into the darkness, listening to the steady
rise and fall of his breathing. Her loins ached and as she
moved restlessly he turned in his sleep pinning her
beneath his arm. It was strong and warm but gentle now
that the rage in him had died. She could have escaped
easily if she tried, but she didn't want to. He was right,
she would stay, for Sophie's sake, but more than that,
because she loved him.

She was wakened early the next morning by the sound of
a servant drawing the curtains and placing a tray with tea
and toast and fresh fruit on the small table beside the
bed. Opening her eyes she stared drowsily at the unfamiliar room then sat up, remembering with horror the
rumpled place in the bed beside her and becoming
conscious of the bruises on her body. But there was no
sign of Brett. With a sudden stab of fear she wondered
where he was. Perhaps the servant would know. But
even as she thought it and tried to frame the words to
ask, the door opened and Brett came into the room. He
seemed scarcely aware of the servant yet he must have
been for he came over to her and kissed her cheek.

'Good morning. I trust you slept well.'

'Yes.' She smiled shyly as he said something to the
servant who salaamed and went out leaving them alone.
Suddenly she felt uncomfortable, remembering what
had happened, and the manner in which it had happened. Did he even remember? 'I'm afraid I must have
overslept. You've been out.' She sipped at the delicately
flavoured tea.

'You didn't oversleep. I woke early and it seemed a
shame to wake you.' He studied her face and she felt her
colour rise as she waited for him to say something.

Instead he turned away, pouring another cup of tea and handing it to her. He was behaving as if nothing had happened, she thought, dully.

'I thought we'd take a carriage and drive into town. I think you'll like it. I'll leave you to get dressed and see you downstairs.'

He was right, it was impossible not to fall in love with it. To Abigail it was like stepping into another world, a world of strange people and movement and noise. A magical blend of colours, sights and smells and, contrary to her expectations, Brett seemed to be going out of his way to make certain she enjoyed every moment of it. That he didn't entirely succeed was not his fault, it was as if the change in their relationship had left her feeling nervous and ill at ease. To have him escort her through the crowded streets, his hand beneath her arm as they toured the sights, to hear herself addressed as Mrs Farraday, were things to which she was sure she would never become accustomed. Yet in spite of it all she felt herself thrilling later to the grandeur of a ball at Government House. Somehow he had arranged it without her knowledge but it was something she would remember for the rest of her life.

The building was white and palatial. Entering its portals she moved instinctively closer to Brett as they were led by liveried servants towards the great ballroom where they were to be introduced to their host and hostess.

Abigail made her curtsy nervously. She had caught only a glimpse of the multitude of figures already whirling about the room and was conscious of the simplicity of her gown of pale rose-coloured satin. Rising from her curtsy, however, she saw not only approval but appreciation in the face of her host. Then they were moving

forward into the mêlée of noise under the brilliance of
glittering chandeliers. She wondered whether Brett
would invite her to dance. The thought of being held
closely in his arms caused her heart to react violently,
but instead he led her through the crowded room, past
the orchestra to a space by an open window. From there
she studied the scene, fascinated yet uneasy.

'Do you know these people?'

'Some of them. Most are members of the Civil Service
or planters. Some are with the army of course.' His
expression darkened. 'They all seem to find the social
round a necessity. Not a view I share.'

'Then why did you bring me here?'

'I thought you might find it interesting. . . amusing.'

It was true, she did find it interesting, the brilliant
colours of the gowns vying with the scarlets and blues of
the uniforms, and yet there was something about it all
which left her with a feeling of distaste. The elegance she
saw here, the gossip, the fluttering of fans, the champagne and mouth-watering food bore no relation to the
things she had seen beyond the town. The poverty out
there was a different world from that lived in by these
people.

She forced herself to smile as they were approached
by two of the guests.

'Farraday, my dear chap, what brings you here? Hardly your cup of tea I'd have thought?' The man's florid
gaze passed to Abigail, disturbing in its appraisal, nor
was that of the over-dressed lady beside him any less
disconcerting. She sensed their curiosity, it would have
been difficult to do otherwise since it was quite blatant,
and she was aware of the ripple of resentment which ran
through her even as her lips formed their stiff smile.
Brett, however, seemed unaware of her discomfort.

'You're right, Harrington, not my cup of tea at all but as this is my wife's first trip to Darjeeling it seemed right she should see the sights.'

'Your wife? Well I'm dashed. Honeymoon, eh?'

Abigail flinched at the sudden coarseness in his tone.

'My dear how marvellous,' Mrs Harrington echoed. 'Though I can't imagine what possesses any woman to come out to this God-forsaken country.' She plied her fan vigorously to her cheeks. 'The natives are thoroughly insolent and quite lazy. Worse still they are utterly heathen. One does one's best of course. You have to be firm. Authority is the only thing they understand isn't that so, Henry?'

'Quite, quite. But you'll soon learn. Give 'em an inch and they take a mile. Got to keep 'em in their place, it's the only way. Can't agree with this idea that they should be educated. What's the point, they haven't the brains for it. Simply gives 'em ideas above their station, don't you agree, Farraday?'

Abigail had to fight the sudden feeling of disgust and anger which welled up in her. She listened only vaguely to what was said, Celia Harrington's voice rising shrilly in her ears until she wanted to cover them, to escape from such bigoted arguments. Surely Brett couldn't share such views. But his expression when she glanced up was totally implacable.

She sipped at her champagne, anger rising within her. Suddenly, beneath all the glitter, something horrid had reared its head.

'But surely these people have more right, if we are honest, to be here than the British?' she heard herself say and felt her cheeks colour as a lengthy silence fell. Celia Harrington's brow rose, her fan fluttered energetically, her thin mouth curving with distaste as her gaze flickered over Abigail.

'My dear Mrs Farraday, if your husband is wise,' her glance flickered to Brett, 'he will advise you to be extremely cautious of expressing such views. You are new to India and so may be excused for not understanding.' Her hand rested on Abigail's arm drawing her aside. 'Believe me, my dear, there are many people who come out here full of ideals only to discover that one simply cannot deal with these natives as if they were ordinary human beings. They are not. Their wretched way of life is the only one they understand or desire.'

Abigail felt as if her mouth was stretched into a taut line. 'I'm afraid I find that very difficult to believe.'

Henry Harrington intervened, 'So do most people when they first come out here, but it's true. What would they do with wealth if they had it? I'll tell you, squander it because they know no better.'

'Then surely it is time someone taught them.' She heard Celia Harrington's sharp gasp of disbelief. Henry Harrington cleared his throat then laughed, obviously ill at ease.

'And what would a chap like me do for workers if we educated 'em? No, Mrs Farraday, I'm afraid you've got a lot to learn, but then a pretty young thing like you don't need to worry her head over it.'

'I'm afraid I should find it very hard to ignore.'

'Then for your own sake I can only advise you to keep such views to yourself,' Celia Harrington said, acidly, 'because you will soon find they will not make you welcome in society. And now, good evening to you.' Her withering glance flickered as she touched her husband's arm and was led away leaving Abigail struggling to contain her temper. She stared defiantly at Brett who had remained infuriatingly silent throughout the exchange.

'I suppose you are very angry, I had no right. . .'

A glint of amusement touched. his eyes. 'On the contrary, you had every right. The Harringtons are the worst kind of advertisement for the British out here. Unfortunately there are too many like them.'

Her eyes widened. 'You really believe that?'

'Haven't I just said so?' He looked down into her troubled face. 'Am I really so like them that you think I share their narrow views?'

She gazed at him, perplexed. 'How am I to know when you never speak to me of how you feel?'

'Then perhaps it's time we did speak of it and many other things.' he said, softly. 'But don't judge everyone by the Harringtons. There are some, a few, who aren't just here for what they can get out of the country before they go back to England.'

She stared round her. 'I'm sure this is all very beautiful and grand but it seems so unreal, so extravagant when there is so much starving and squalor everywhere.'

He took the glass from her hand. 'Perhaps it was a mistake to bring you here. I thought you might enjoy it. It seems I was wrong.'

'No, I am. . .'

'You don't lie very convincingly, Abby.' The words were spoken very softly against her ear and before she knew what was happening his arms were about her and they were dancing. Her feet seemed to be moving by some guidance other than her own. The very fact of being in his arms, of being held close, seemed to have driven every conscious thought out of her body. She was only aware that they moved together as if completely attuned and that she never wanted the music to end.

Refreshments were served during the course of the evening. Her plate was filled and she picked at the delicacies but her head ached and she wanted nothing more than to escape. But there were more introductions to be made, more hands to be shaken, more congratulations to be received and smiled at as if for all the world she was a young bride enjoying her first entry into society.

It was a relief when she looked into the sympathetic face of Helen Rydall, the wife of a tea planter. Abigail took an instant liking to the woman whose features, though still attractive, bore the inevitable stamp of someone who had lived a number of years in India's savage climate. Already she was discovering that it was not kind to women.

Side by side they wandered out on to the terrace leaving the men to talk. It was refreshing to discover that not everyone shared the Harringtons' opinions and after a while she could even laugh about it.

'I'm afraid I've already been warned that my outspokenness will certainly mean I shall be ostracised by society,' she confessed.

Helen Rydall laughed. 'You mustn't take it too seriously. I had the very same warnings when I first came out to India and that was ten years ago. I can assure you, my dear, that though I was certainly starry-eyed as all new brides are, as you yourself are, my views haven't changed.' She frowned. 'I don't make the mistake of thinking things will change overnight or that I can personally affect the thinking of a whole generation, but gradually, change must come. I'm afraid the British aren't the saviours they believe themselves to be. A great many of them, people like the Harringtons, are here only for what they can get out of India and having bled the land and people dry, they will go back to England. Their kind we can do without. Unfortunately it is often the others who go, the ones we can ill do without.' She smiled. 'Forgive me for saying it but you come as something of a surprise. We had no idea. After Elaina we didn't imagine. . .' She broke off.

'You knew Elaina?' Abigail felt her heartbeat quicken.

'Our paths crossed.' Helen stared out into the darkness of the night. 'She was quite extraordinarily beautiful. It was easy to see why Brett fell in love with her as he did.'

'Yes, so I believe.' Abigail felt stifled. She was glad of the darkness which hid her misery and it was a relief when the men came out at that moment to join them and the talk became general once again. Shortly before they said their farewells she turned impulsively to Helen. 'Please, come to Mandara if ever you can manage it.'

'Yes,' Helen kissed her cheek, 'I should like that.'

It was a promise to which Abigail clung, feeling that at last she had one friend.

As they drove back in the carriage to the hotel she broke the silence to ask tentatively, 'I trust you have no objections to my inviting Mrs Rydall to visit? I'm afraid I didn't think. . . it didn't occur to me that you might not wish it.

For some reason his tone was curt. 'My dear Abby, Mandara is now as much yours as it is mine. You must do as you please, there is no need to ask my approval.'

'Thank you.' Frowning she turned from him to stare out of the window, clenching her hands in her lap. His indifference hit her like a wave of cold water. How she would endure the rest of their honeymoon she didn't know. Without realising it she sighed.

'Would you prefer to return home, Abby?'

Surprised she looked at him. It was impossible to keep the relief from her voice. 'You. . . you mean it?'

'Of course,' he frowned. 'Would I have asked it otherwise? But I think there is no need for you to give me an answer.'

Her gaze fell before his. 'Yes, I would like to go. . . back to Mandara.' She couldn't bring herself to call it home for the word somehow conjured up too many things which could never be possible, but she felt the stirring of excitement in the pit of her stomach.

A faint smile touched his lips. 'It hasn't exactly been successful has it? Perhaps I should have known better than to expect it could be.'

For some reason her heart felt like a lead weight in her breast. Known better than to think he could ever forget Elaina, she thought. She would never set him free. 'No,' she said quietly. 'Perhaps we should both have known better.'

CHAPTER
ELEVEN

WITHIN minutes of their return Sophie was enthusiastically tearing the wrappings from the new gown they had brought back with them as a gift for her, her cries of delight at their return doubled by a sight of the exquisite little creation in white tulle and pink rosebuds. Having danced around the room with the dress clasped to her, displaying an already amazingly feminine love of pretty things, she ran to try it on and enjoy the ecstatic approval of her doting *ayah*.

Abigail watched her go, smiling. She was glad they had returned. This was normality, or at least as normal as she could expect from now on in her life as Brett's wife.

Their trunks were still being unloaded from the carriage when she heard Brett order the *syce* to have his horse saddled and brought round. Puzzled she said, 'Are you going out so soon? But we've only just arrived, won't Sophie expect to see something of you?' Then she bit her lip, aware that it had sounded almost like a wifely reproof and that she had no right to query his actions. But if he noticed it he gave no sign.

'I know we've only just returned but I want to go to the mine. I'm afraid you're going to have to get used to my being away. If there's anything you need, ask Gopal. He knows Mandara as well as I do, he'll deal with any questions you have.'

Crushed, she drew back. If he had chosen to remind

her that she was a stranger here he couldn't have made it more plain, or was she merely being over-sensitive? She watched him go, feeling confused and a little afraid. Within minutes of their return she was discovering that though Mandara was the same, everything else had changed. Her position there was no longer that of Sophie's companion, she was mistress here, but a mistress as yet without any authority.

She stood in the hall easing off her gloves as she looked about her, aware that the servants were regarding her warily. She could tell by their glances that they were afraid the new memsahib would wish to make changes and upset their easy-going routine. The British ladies had a reputation for wishing to sweep clean with new brooms, turning upside down everything which had been so comfortably settled. The *punkah-wallah* stirred himself in the corner where he had fallen into a comfortable doze and began to work the fan, stirring up a waft of warm air which brought little and only temporary relief before his eyes closed again and the movement gradually ceased.

Gopal's foot roused him sharply and the man shrank beneath a verbal lashing which made Abigail feel sorry for the cowering man.

'He is a lazy good for nothing fellow,' Gopal assured her, 'and he will take advantage. It is best to deal most severely, it is all a fellow like that understands.'

Abigail listened, at first in amusement and then in dismay. Only now were the full implications of the responsibilities she had assumed beginning to dawn upon her. She had never had the ordering of a household of servants before, she knew nothing of which servant was responsible for which tasks, but Gopal was right. He had tried to show her, as tactfully as possible, that she must have the courage to assert her authority as if she had been accustomed all her life to it. It was after all only what any army wife would have to learn from the moment she set foot in this country.

She drew herself up. There had been two sides to the bargain. She must keep hers. 'I think I am going to need your help Gopal, there is a great deal I have to learn.'

'I am honoured to be of assistance to the memsahib.'

The words were spoken with a sincerity which touched her deeply and she wondered how she could ever have doubted that he had wanted anything other than her husband's happiness. It was ironic, she thought, that they both shared the same desire. It forged some kind of bond between them and suddenly she was glad of it.

'You will have to show me what is expected,' she said quietly.

He held out a bunch of keys attached to a chain. 'It is right the memsahib should now take these.'

As she stared at the keys relinquished into her hand she realised that she knew very little of the house of which she was now mistress.

Slowly Gopal led her from room to room, throwing open doors, allowing her to step inside each room before closing it again. Automatically she went to the next, fittting a key to the lock. It didn't fit and she tried another then another, finally looking up just in time to see a troubled frown disfigure Gopal's features.

'There doesn't seem to be a key for this room. Is it lost?'

For an instant his glance fell away. 'No, memsahib, it is not lost, but the sahib, he keeps it about his person. No one is permitted to enter or touch the belongings of the first memsahib.'

Stunned, she let her hand fall. She couldn't trust

herself to speak and swallowed convulsively instead. So this was his shrine to Elaina. His love for her had consumed him and her betrayal had filled him with a bitterness so strong that nothing could penetrate it, yet still he couldn't break free. Abigail turned blindly away. Brett could no more escape the past than she could the future. They were bound together inextricably and somehow she must find the strength to bear it. Her eyes closed as a sob broke from her.

'Be patient, memsahib,' Gopal's voice reminded her gently of his presence. 'All will be well.'

She drew herself up, ashamed that he should have witnessed her naked despair. 'Will it, Gopal? Will it?'

'I have known the sahib for many years, since he was a child. I have seen him fight many battles. He is strong.'

Yes, he was strong. She moved away, her skirts rustling, but was the memory of Elaina and the hurt she had inflicted even stronger? It seemed it was and it would be better if she could accept it rather than hope.

Abigail noticed a subtle change in the weather as the days passed. The heat was even greater despite the wind which now seemed to come in great, scorching blasts which tore at the lungs. Even sleep became impossible.

Time hung heavily too, for all she tried to fill it, searching for tasks only to have a servant immediately appear to remove it from her more than willing hands, leaving her once again idle and resentful. Very quickly she came to realise that her intrusions were as unwelcome as they were unfitting the wife of the sahib. She learned that to be mistress of the house meant she had only to issue orders which would be carried out by the servants under the ever-watchful eyes of Gopal. It was neither expected nor encouraged that she should soil her hands with any task, however slight or menial. In desperation she even made an attempt at gardening but when she requested that the dead flowers and debris be removed and burned she was met by wails of protest until she held her head, wishing she could shut out the noise of the boy who threw himself to the ground before her, wailing and raising his hands to the sky. All her entreaties would not remove him. It was Gopal who finally drove him away, speaking sharply before he turned to explain.

'It is not this fellow's place to perform such tasks, memsahib.'

'But I only asked him to remove this debris.'

'Indeed. I will have it attended to, memsahib.'

And so, miserably, she even abandoned the garden, wondering whether she would ever learn. Caste was everything to these people. Even in the kitchens all was not straightforward. The menus were brought to her each morning for her decision but no matter what choices she made, the cook somehow always contrived to serve chicken, and that always highly flavoured with curry, which, though she found the flavour subtle and enjoyable to begin with, soon began to become boring.

It wasn't even as if she had Brett's company to break the monotony. He invariably left the house before dawn and wouldn't return until late, by which time she had eaten her own meal in solitary silence.

At first she had taken special pains to dress for the occasion. Now, although she still made the effort, there was no pleasure in it only to sit at the table, staring the length of it to the empty seat at the far end. She wondered if he was purposely avoiding her. Was this what he had meant when he had said they would each remain free to lead their own lives? If so, then it was a kind of cruelty she couldn't understand until a voice seemed to whisper in her ear, like an echo crying from the past. Had Elaina also sat here, day after day, night after night, waiting for the husband who never came? Had she too finally been able to bear it no longer?

Abigail pressed a hand to her head, rising quickly to leave the table. Perhaps it was because she had been so deep in thought that she had failed to hear the sound of his footsteps and she gasped to see him standing there before her so suddenly.

Lines of exhaustion were etched deeply into his dust-covered face. She watched in silence as he unfastened his jacket, throwing it aside, then she moved to pour some wine, holding the glass out to him. He took it saying nothing and his silence troubled her, banishing the momentary joy she had felt at seeing him.

'Would you like some food? I'm afraid I've already eaten but Gopal. . .'

'No.' He shook his head closing his eyes. 'I don't want anything.'

'What has happened?' she asked, quietly. 'Something is wrong, won't you tell me? Surely I have at least that right?'

'Of course you have the right.' Anger exploded from him as he wiped a hand across his brow. 'I assumed you wouldn't be interested.'

'Of course I'm interested. I've waited for hours, wondering what had happened to you.'

He stared at her, leaning back in his chair, his hand covering his mouth as he studied her, and she was glad that for some reason she had lingered more carefully than usual upon her choice of gown. It was simple yet elegant, green satin shot through with shades of blue.

For a moment she sensed his approval then he leaned forward letting his hand fall.

'I lost another man today.'

'Oh no! How?'

'His neck was broken. It looks as if he fell but the workers either can't or won't believe that.' Getting to his feet he refilled his glass. 'Perhaps they're right, it's me that's jinxed. Perhaps I should pull out.'

Her reaction was instinctive. 'But you can't. Surely you don't believe that. You mustn't.' Her hand was on his arm. 'The mine is your life, everything you've worked for.'

Briefly he stared at it and at her and she was shocked by the disillusionment in his eyes. 'I used to think that. Now I wonder. Anyway, I may not have a choice much longer.'

'What do you mean?'

He shrugged. 'No men, no mine. I don't think I can hold them together much longer and even if I can the monsoons are beginning.'

'I don't understand.'

He lifted his glass, gesturing to something beyond her. 'After the monsoon, the rains. I've got to get the river dammed before they start or I'll have a raging torrent wiping out the whole thing.'

Her throat tightened. 'What will you do?'

'I don't have a choice.'

His back was to her, rigid and unyielding despite his exhaustion. She wanted to go to him, to put her arms about him, offer what meagre comfort she could. But he didn't want her comfort, he wanted nothing she could offer. Her fists clenched.

'You're tired, you should get some rest.'

He turned and the breath caught in her throat as he

looked at her. She tried to read the expression in his eyes but the lights on the terrace cast distorting shadows over everything, except the need in her own heart.

'Shall I leave you?'

For a moment she thought he hadn't heard then he frowned. 'There is no need.'

'If my presence troubles you. . .'

'It doesn't.' His fingers probed the throbbing behind his eyes.

'I wish I could help. I am your wife, I should like to feel I could at least do something. . .' She broke off, helplessly, then miraculously she saw him reach out, his hand on her arm drawing her closer.

'God knows, I wish. . .' He shook his head, then with a muttered oath his lips came down on hers, gently at first then savagely, bruising her eager mouth until the breath was driven from her lungs. She clung to him. drowning in the ecstasy of her emotions, not daring to ask why, not even caring. She moaned softly as his hand caressed her neck, her back, moulding her to him, demanding. The sound became a sob as her senses cried out for fulfilment, her head tilted back, eyes closed, as he released her mouth at last. She heard him murmur something and her lashes flickered open as he put her abruptly from him.

The colour drained from her face, her fingers going to her naked shoulders where his hands had disturbed her gown. Shame twisted like a knife in her breast. How could she have allowed herself to forget, even for an instant? In a moment of weakness he had turned to her and she had succumbed to the desires of her own body. But it was not herself he had needed, it was Elaina, and his savagery had not been passion but anger.

Her hand trembled against her mouth as she backed

away from the look in his eyes. 'I. . . forgive me.' She turned to stumble from the room avoiding his suddenly out-thrust hand.

She lay for a long time on her bed staring up at the net as it moved gently above her in the cooler night air. Somehow she had forced her shaking hands to unfasten her gown and had stepped out of it, leaving it where it fell. Her body felt bruised but that was nothing compared to the dull ache which throbbed deep inside her.

She lay awake for a long time. Only as the hours passed did she admit to herself that Brett wasn't going to come to her and, biting back a sob, she flung an arm across her face in an attempt to blot out the memory of her first surrender, even whilst she knew it would be imprinted on her brain for ever.

The air was stifling. Wind stirred the curtains against the open window but still she couldn't breathe, and after a while she thrust the net aside and got up. The rain-bearing winds of the monsoon were driving down from the north, venting their rage against the Himalayas until they reached the lower hills and desert plains where they would finally expend themselves as rain. *If* the rain came. It was strange that something as simple as water could be taken for granted yet, out here, it was the very life blood of the people. Only now did she begin to understand what the failure of the monsoon could mean in terms of tragedy and human suffering.

Restlessly she made her way to Sophie's room where she closed the shutters and went to stand for a moment beside the bed. The child was sleeping peacefully, the dark hair curled damply against the pillow. She bent quickly to kiss the flushed face which was a smaller image of that other, then left, closing the door gently behind her. Sophie was happy, that was all that mattered. Nothing else was important.

She was making her way back to the bedroom when a sound disturbed her, bringing her to a halt. Brett? Her heart leapt, then she froze. Someone was moving in the darkness. She heard a faint rustling, caught the merest waft of perfume, elusive yet somehow disturbingly familiar. She drew back quickly into the shadows. Who would be moving about the house at this hour of night and why? Even the servants would be asleep by now.

Rigid with sudden fear she stood pressed against the wall. The figure moved, so close that if she had reached out a hand she might have touched it. She heard a faint tapping, a door opened and the figure moved again, silhouetted briefly against the light of a lamp. Abigail held her breath. It was the room which had always been kept locked, which she was not allowed to enter. Elaina's room.

Abigail had to press a hand to her mouth to stifle a scream as she recognised Gita and then, as she watched, another figure moved into view. She held her breath. Ice-cold with shock she heard Brett's voice. The girl made some answer then, slowly, as if at some invitation, she moved slowly into the room and into Brett's arms. Her hands drew his face down to her own in a kiss before the door swung softly to a close.

CHAPTER
TWELVE

IT WAS dawn before Abigail finally slept, only to be woken again by the sound of Brett riding away from the house. She had no way of knowing when Gita had left but mercifully there was no sign of the girl when eventually she made her way downstairs.

For once even Sophie's chatter seemed to set her nerves on edge as they sat at the table. She tried to respond but her head ached and there were deep shadows beneath her eyes, shadows she was glad Brett was not there to see.

Her gaze went dully to the silver dish beside her plate. A letter lay on it, the first she had received since coming out to India and at first she stared at the name written on it before recognising that Mrs Brett Farraday was herself. She opened it. It was from Helen Rydall, proposing herself for a visit. At any other time she would have welcomed the suggestion but now. . . She put the letter aside realising that Sophie had been speaking and was waiting expectantly for an answer.

'What. . . oh yes, of course you can ride today, provided you wear your hat and you promise to do as *ayah* tells you.'

'Oh I shall, I shall. We're going for a picnic up into the hills, it will be cooler up there.'

Abigail's glance went hesitantly to Gopal. 'Is it perfectly safe?'

He bowed. 'The *syce* is a good man, memsahib, he will

ensure it for he will accompany the little one.'

'Well then I see no reason why not.'

With a cry of delight Sophie abandoned her unfinished breakfast and ran to prepare for the outing, leaving Abigail to push away her own plate and reach for more coffee. It was strong and reviving but did nothing to ease her depression. Setting her cup down she went through the motions of folding her napkin.'

'Where is Gita this morning, I haven't seen her.'

'Gita, memsahib?' For a moment Gopal's features held a wariness she had not seen before. 'I do not know, memsahib.'

The answer seemed to stir a spark of anger within her as she sensed that he lied. Wisdom told her not to pursue the matter, but she no longer cared for what was wise. She rose to her feet. 'I think you do know, Gopal. What are you keeping from me? Is she in this house?'

His glance fell as he shook his head, 'Oh no, memsahib.'

'I see.' The words almost choked her but she forced herself to go on. 'But you know that she was here last night, just as you know everything that happens in this house.' She forestalled his protest even before it rose, watching him and seeing the sadness in his eyes as they lifted to meet her own. But she had to know the truth, all of it, so that never again would she be tempted to give way to any weakness. Her chin rose. 'How long has she been coming to. . . to my husband?'

He wailed softly, 'Please, memsahib. . .'

'Don't you see, I have to know. You know that my place in this house is not. . . as it should be. I don't question it, I am fully aware of what I am committed to, but I must know, for his sake and mine, so that I can make no mistakes. Is Gita still my husband's mistress?'

A look of pleading came into the bearer's eyes. 'It means nothing, memsahib.'

'I want the truth.'

His hands gestured. 'In my country where many white men have no wives, or their women have gone into the hills for the summer, it happens that a man will seek consolation elsewhere, but these things do not last, memsahib. With the memsahib's return such associations end and no harm is done.' He watched, silently, as she turned and left him rather than let him see the pain his words had inflicted.

The fact that she had none of the rights of an ordinary wife only made the torment all the more real somehow. How could she remain in this house as his wife, knowing that he shared his bed with another woman? They had made a bargain but she had not imagined he would be so cruel as to make this a part of it.

Tears made a blur of the brilliant reds and blues of the flowers around her. She had to get away, to be alone, to think. Hurrying to her room she changed into a riding skirt and blouse, carrying her hat as she ran to the courtyard where the *syce* had her horse saddled and waiting. He moved to follow her but she dismissed him, for once ignoring his protests of alarm. She had to be alone. Jerkily her hands grasped the reins and she gave the animal its head.

She rode hard, punishing both herself and her mount, not even conscious of the direction she took. Her skirts billowed against the side-saddle, at one moment she was almost unseated as the animal stumbled but she pulled him up, urging him still faster. Her hair pulled free of its pins as the wind drove hot and relentless towards her but she didn't stop, wanting to go on for ever, up into the distant hills and the blissful shade of the trees. In the distance, snow-covered mountain peaks towered, and, as if sensing her need, the horse responded.

She didn't see the branch which lay broken and twisted across the track. The animal lurched and with one small cry Abigail was flung off to hang suspended for a second in mid-air before hitting the ground with a violence which drove the breath sickeningly from her lungs. A searing pain shot through her arm like a blade tearing into the flesh. She screamed, then everything seemed to be whirling about her, the sky, the trees, like a deep, dark whirlpool. She tried to sit up only to feel herself falling yet again into a blackness which enveloped her, blotting out everything.

The voice came to her from a long way off. It intruded upon her pain and semi-consciousness and she moaned softly as it dragged her ruthlessly out of the merciful blackness. Her eyelids flickered and a figure moved, blotting out the sun, raising her carefully as he held a flask to her lips. The water was warm and brackish and she coughed as it trickled down her throat, before pushing it away and lying back as she tried to remember what had happened.

'It's Miss Tarrant, isn't it?'

Movement sent a shaft of pain through her again and she hugged her injured arm to her, nodding. 'Yes, it is but. . .' She couldn't think. 'Where am I?'

'Don't try to sit up, at least not for a minute or two. You were thrown from your horse. It's lucky I came along.' He tipped water from the flask onto his handkerchief, pressing it to her forehead where a small trickle of blood ran, matting her hair.

There was something vaguely familiar about his features and about his voice which her mind couldn't place.

They swam and receded beneath the waves of dizziness, then gradually the mist cleared. 'Mr Peters.' Relief brought the tears to her eyes as she smiled up at him. 'You seem to make a habit of coming to my rescue.'

'I'm only too happy to oblige, though I wish we could meet under somewhat different circumstances.'

Slowly, carefully, she managed to sit up and look around her. 'How long have I been here?'

'Not long. I heard you scream and came across your horse making for the river.'

'Oh no, is he hurt?'

'I'm afraid he's limping. I've tethered him over there. I was more concerned to see that you were alive before I tended to the animal.'

Abigail struggled awkwardly to her feet, leaning heavily on him as another bout of giddiness swept over her. It passed but she still felt weak and shaky. 'I must get back, I shall be missed.'

'Well I'm afraid you can't ride that animal, that's for sure, and even if it were possible I doubt if you're in any fit state at this moment to stay in the saddle.'

Anxiety clouded her eyes. 'But what am I to do?'

James Peters' glance lingered on the paleness of her face and for a moment a vague uneasiness stirred in her. It was banished as he smiled.

'There's no problem. I'll take you back to my place where you can rest for a while and have that shoulder seen to, then I'll loan you a fresh mount.'

It sounded logical, yet she hesitated as Brett's warning that she keep away from the Peters' place flashed into her mind. She dismissed it as being merely yet another example of his brutish, unreasonable behaviour. In any case, it seemed she scarcely had a choice. 'At least it will give me an opportunity to pay my respects to your sister

at long last,' she said and felt the faint flush of colour rise
in her cheeks. 'I have meant to do so but. . .'

'Please don't apologise.' He brushed away her stam-
mered protests quickly as he led her to his horse, lifted
her into the saddle and pulled himself up easily behind
her. As they rode she was conscious of his arm about her
and his face close, a shade too close to her own. She
stiffened and drew away, holding her body rigid, but he
seemed not to notice, and after a while she was even
quite glad to have him there as nausea and dizziness
began to envelop her again. Then his grip tightened
about her, almost imperceptibly.

By the time they reached his bungalow, her shoulder
was throbbing so badly that she allowed herself to be
carried into the cool interior and settled on a couch.
Vaguely she was aware of James Peters giving softly
spoken orders to a sikh boy who returned moments later
with a tray bearing a jug of fresh lemonade and a glass
which he placed on a small table beside her. She sipped
at the drink slowly, gradually taking in her surroundings
as James followed the boy out. Putting the glass down
she closed her eyes, hearing the lowered voices but
paying no attention to them. The pain of her shoulder
seemed to be having a strange effect upon her, making
her want to drift into sleep. But she mustn't let that
happen, she had to get back.

Her gaze took in the brightly coloured rugs scattered
about the bungalow, and the furnishings, most of which
had undoubtedly been shipped from England. Indeed,
even the gardens, so neatly laid out with lawns and beds
of flowers, invoked a memory of the English countryside.

She looked up as he returned and realised that he
wasn't as good-looking as she had thought that day in

Bombay when he had first come to her aid. In fact there was a distinct suggestion of weakness to the line of his chin and jaw, a hint of dissipation in the eyes which studied her, half smiling now. She put her feet to the floor, suddenly uneasy, though not knowing why.

'I dread to think what Miss Peters will think if she sees me like this. Perhaps I could tidy myself a little before meeting her?'

He was pouring a drink and turned as she spoke, a slightly rueful smile flickering across his face. 'Ah, well as a matter of fact, Miss Tarrant, my sister isn't here at this moment.'

'Not here?' Ignoring the glass he held out to her she stared at him, the feeling of unease increasing. 'But surely you said. . .'

'No. Of course I should have explained but I didn't think you were really in any state to take it in.' His laughter sounded false and he refused to meet her gaze. 'Agnes is visiting friends who have only just come out from England. Felt it her duty to help get them settled, you know how it is?'

Abigail rose unsteadily to her feet, not knowing at all how it was, but forcing a smile rather than let him see the apprehension she was really feeling. 'I see. Well I am sorry, but at least next time I shall be able to pay my respects formally to her instead of arriving like this.' She held out her torn, dust-stained skirts ruefully. 'I really would like to freshen up before returning to Mandara and then I must leave. You've been most kind but I'm feeling much better, truly.' Her glance rose to find him watching her. He still stood, glass in hand, making no move.

'There is to be a next time then?'

Abigail felt herself grow suddenly rigid with dislike. It

was only now that she recognised the feeling for what it was, and that accompanying it was a growing sense of fear. She shouldn't have come here. He had deliberately misled her into believing his sister would be at home, surely realising that she might otherwise have refused. And yet what choice had she had? He was right, she wouldn't have been capable of riding back to Mandara.

Nervously she gathered up her riding crop. 'Perhaps Miss Peters will send me a note when she returns.'

He drained his glass and set it down. 'You mean to stay then?'

'Stay?'

'At Mandara.'

Her fingers felt the drumming of the pulse at her throat. But of course, he didn't know. . . 'Yes, I intend to remain.'

'I see.' He gaze narrowed appreciatively. 'Well there's no point in my denying the fact that I'm glad. Perhaps we shall have the opportunity to become better acquainted?'

Unable to bear the narrow scrutiny she moved away, edging towards the door.

'Yes indeed. I'm sure you must be looking forward to your wife's return, Mr Peters.'

There was a moment's silence during which he seemed grimly amused. 'To be honest, Miss Tarrant, I don't think that's very likely. But of course,' he saw her mouth open, 'I told you she had stayed behind in England to see our daughter into school and that was true. What I neglected to say was that she has no intention of returning to India.'

'I. . . I see, and I'm sorry.' She was shocked to hear him laugh.

'Oh I assure you I don't need your sympathy, Miss

Tarrant. Olivia's going was the best thing that's happened to me in a long time. I'm only surprised she stayed as long as she did in view of the fact that she always maintained it was a hell on earth. The fact that she made it a hell for me had little or no bearing on it.' He shrugged. 'But don't let that prevent you coming by whenever you wish.'

Abigail recoiled involuntarily as his fingers brushed lightly against her arm. 'I must go.'

'Now I've shocked you.'

She tried to back away but her legs seemed incapable of fitting the action to the thought. 'Yes, I am shocked, because you brought me here under false pretences.'

'Oh surely not so, Miss Tarrant, you were only too glad of my help.'

'But you must have known I would have refused if I had known . . .'

His brow rose, his face suddenly surly, frightening. 'What difference does it make?'

'All the difference in the world. Surely if you are a gentleman you can see that.'

'I'm afraid I don't, but then, I've never claimed to be a gentleman.' He laughed softly. 'Far too inhibiting. In any case, I think you're forgetting something.'

'I don't understand.'

'How do you intend getting back to Mandara? Your horse is lame, you can scarcely walk in this heat. I think, Miss Tarrant, you need my help.'

She took a deep breath. 'Are you saying that you refuse to give it?'

'Not at all. I'm simply saying that you might have died out there. Surely I deserve a little thanks . . . a reward for coming to the rescue. Don't you agree?'

She backed away from him, her gaze widening with

horror as his meaning became clear, but he came closer, his eyes glinting dangerously. 'I. . . I am grateful for what you did.'

'Grateful.' He laughed softly. 'Well that's very handsome of you, Miss Tarrant, but not exactly what I had in mind.'

She knew she must stay calm, or at least maintain an impression of calm. 'There is something you don't know, something I should explain, you see I am married.'

'Married?' Her words seemed to stop him in his tracks.

'Yes, I. . . I am married to Brett Farraday. I am his wife.'

For an instant shock registered in his eyes then he swore under his breath. 'His wife, by God, that's rich.'

With a sense of shock she realised that far from deterring him, her words had somehow only served to increase his determination and before she could move, his hand had closed over her wrist. She struggled furiously, beating at him with the riding crop until he thrust it away.

'Please, let me go.'

'Oh I will, but first let's settle the account a little shall we, Mrs Farraday, it's long overdue.' She didn't understand and had no time to wonder as his mouth closed on hers, his hands moving over her body in a way which sent shivers of terror and disgust running through her. She fought violently, hampered by the pain in her shoulder. Her breath came in sobs but he was crushing her relentlessly against his powerful frame, the smell of spirit on his breath sending a wave of nausea through her. Blindly she lashed out, clawing at his face with her nails. Shock and pain forced him to release her just for a second, but it was enough. Sobbing she dragged herself from his grasp as he reeled, a hand clutched to his face where blood trickled slowly down his cheek. But she didn't stay to see what damage she had inflicted. She ran, stumbling over her skirt, her hand jarring against the door frame as she fled down the steps to where James Peters' own horse was still saddled and tethered. Snatching the reins, somehow she managed to find the strength to haul herself up into the saddle, gasping as the shock of pain almost caused her to pass out, but knowing that she mustn't, not now, not here. Her heels dug into the animal's flanks just as Peters came stumbling down the steps towards her. He reached out but was too slow as she urged the horse forward, brushing against him and seeing him spin away.

She had no way of knowing how long she rode or how far, even whether she was heading in the right direction. The sun beat mercilessly down on her head and vaguely she remembered that her hat still lay on the couch where she had left it. It didn't seem to matter.

After a while she slowed the horse to a walking pace, instinctively following ground which began to seem vaguely familiar. Of course, she had ridden this way with Brett when he had brought her to see the mine. The thought of him made her slump in the saddle, the tears which had until now been held in check falling at last. Where was he now? Why had she been so foolish as to disobey him?

The landscape became blurred and her thoughts seemed to be circling, just as the sky was circling above her head. It was strange how, even in her state of delirium, she could actually get the feeling that he was there. Even as she slipped from the saddle someone caught and held her, mumuring her name.

It was only as she allowed herself to open her eyes that

she realised he was reality and no dream, that she was
lying on the ground and he was brushing her forehead,
his face white and filled with an expression she had never
seen before. It was some moments before she remembered her torn gown and the bruises.

'In God's name what happened. Who did this?'

She gasped as she realised what he was thinking. 'I
fell. It was an accident, my horse threw me.'

'This isn't your horse.' His gaze tore itself from her
face to the animal which was grazing close by.

She shook her head, more afraid of his anger than she
had been of James Peters yet not knowing why. 'It
belongs to Peters. He found me and . . .' She couldn't
go on, the memory of what had happened sickened her,
but Brett was shaking her, his face grim.

'And? My God what happened? Tell me.'

A sob broke convulsively from her. 'It was my own
fault, I didn't know. . .' She missed the look which
blazed into his eyes as, for a moment, he thrust her
away. He knelt, his head turned away, and brushed a
hand across his mouth, then he bent and lifted her. He
said nothing and his coldness was even more frightening
than if he had hurt her physically because she couldn't
understand it. She tried to speak, to explain, but he
lifted her into the saddle, and as he rode back with her to
Mandara she knew that she had good reason to be afraid
of what he intended to do.

Gopal was waiting when they returned, his face anxious
as Brett lifted her down from the saddle.

'Please, I can walk. I'm not hurt, only bruised and
very thirsty.'

Without argument he set her on her feet, as if he
couldn't bear to have her near him. He spoke sharply to

Gopal. She didn't understand the words but she saw the bearer's eyes widen as he answered, his gaze flicking to her white face and the state of her clothing.

'Go into the house.'

She shivered at his tone and turned dully towards the steps. The sight of Helen Rydall's figure standing there was so unexpected and so welcome that with a sob she flew to the outstretched arms. At a glance the woman took in her appearance and Brett's grim face. She realised that something was terribly wrong but wasted no time with questions. Instead she hurried Abigail to her room, issuing orders to the servants to bring hot water and linaments.

On the stairs Abigail stopped, calling out as her husband strode grimly away. He neither paused nor looked in her direction and Helen gently put an arm about her.

'Let him go, my dear. We must get these cuts and bruises of yours seen to. In this climate it doesn't pay to hesitate.' Her own face was pale as she helped Abigail to step out of the torn gown and she felt the girl flinch as she began, as carefully as possible, to tend the wounds.

Abigail felt sick. 'I should have stopped Brett, tried to explain.'

'My dear, I doubt that you could have done. I've known Brett for many years and I've never seen him like this. What happened, can you tell me?'

Abigail shook her head weakly. 'It all seems too much like a bad dream. I. . . I fell from my horse. It was my own fault, I was riding crazily, but I just had to get away for a while.' She brushed a hand across her forehead. 'I suppose I must have been stunned, it was probably for no more than a few seconds but when I came to my senses James Peters was bending over me.'

Helen Rydall's voice was suddenly taut, uneven, 'You say. . . Peters?'

'Yes.' Abigail nodded. 'I was lucky, at least I thought so at the time.' She laughed bitterly, a sob catching in her throat. 'My horse was lame, certainly there was no way I could ride him, and when Peters suggested I return with him to his bungalow to recover and find a fresh mount, there didn't seem to be any alternative.' Her stricken gaze flew up to the older woman's. 'Brett warned me to keep away, but he'd never said why and I couldn't have walked back to Mandara even if I had known which direction to take.'

'My dear, I see you had no choice.'

'But will Brett?' Abigail stared dully at her hand clasped comfortingly in the other woman's. 'I blame myself for not suspecting. . . I should have done, there was something about Peters, the way he looked at me.' She shivered. 'But I told myself I was being foolish, that I was more shaken by the fall than I realised and it was making me fanciful. And he led me to believe that his sister would be there.' Her hand clenched. 'It wasn't until I arrived there that I realised he had lied, but by then of course it was too late. Oh, he tried to pass it off, as if I had misunderstood, but she had gone to stay with friends. . .'

Helen rose to her feet. 'My dear, James Peters' sister died three years ago, of the cholera, so you see, I'm afraid he lied to you right from the start.'

Abigail's face whitened. 'But. . . I don't understand. Why?'

'Can you tell me what happened?'

Abigail pressed a hand to her eyes. 'He began to behave strangely, suggesting I visit him. . . but I realised then that of course he didn't know I was Brett's wife.

How could he, it was all so sudden.' Her lips compressed. 'I told him.'

'And?' Helen was watching her closely.

'It was as if he had suddenly gone mad. He laughed and said that it was rich. None of it made sense, and then he. . .he. . .'

'You don't need to go on.' Helen came to sit beside her again, frowning. 'My dear, surely you must know the reason for what happened and for Brett's behaviour?'

Abigail stared at her, uncomprehending. 'What do you mean, what reason could there possibly be?'

'You say Brett warned you to keep away from the Peters' place.'

'Why yes, but it seemed unreasonable. Because there was some kind of feud between them seemed no reason why *I* should have to ignore our neighbours.'

'Dear God, what a fool Brett is!' Helen broke off. 'He should have told you. You of all people had a right to know.'

'To know what,' suddenly Abigail scarcely dared to ask the question, yet she had to know the answer. 'To know what?'

The woman's hand rose as if a spasm had gripped it. 'My dear, forgive me. After Elaina. . . everyone knew, but of course you couldn't, unless Brett told you.'

Abigail felt as if an icy hand had gripped her. She had to swallow hard in order to speak. 'After Elaina what? What should I know?'

The older woman's face contorted. Abigail saw the reluctance in her eyes and went to her, pleading.

'Please, if you are my friend, tell me about Elaina. She is like a ghost haunting me. Even though she is dead, she is still here in this house. I can't escape her, neither can Brett. He still loves her, there is no room in his heart for

anyone else and there never can be. I was a fool to think
it could ever be otherwise, but I must know.'

Shock was mirrored in Helen Rydall's eyes. 'But you
are wrong. Believe me, any love he had for Elaina was
dead within a few months of the marriage. She killed it as
surely as she killed him, in spirit if not in reality.'

'I don't. . . I don't understand. He drove her away.'

'No, my dear, no.' Helen shook her head. 'Elaina
wanted to own him body and soul, but even that was not
enough. She wanted Brett and Mandara but she also
wanted the kind of life he could never give her, and when
she found he couldn't she looked elsewhere, to someone
who could, to James Peters. She was his mistress, everyone knew it.'

Abigail pressed a hand to her mouth, stifling her cry of
horror. 'No, it can't be true.'

'I'm afraid it is. She destroyed Brett, a little at a time,
and we who knew him then could only watch it happen.
There was nothing we could do. Finally of course he
learned the truth. It was inevitable, Elaina was neither
subtle nor discreet. These things happen out here, I
won't deny that. The circumstances under which most
husbands and wives live aren't normal by any standards
we know in England, but one thing has always been
the rule—discretion. Affairs were neither serious nor
flaunted, but Elaina didn't abide by the rules. Oh, she
tried to win him back, she was afraid of the disgrace.'
Helen held Abigail's outflung hand, saw her try to
speak. 'Yes, Brett loved her, desperately, but all that
died and afterwards he was a totally different man. He
has never let another woman come near him since, not in
any real sense of the word, until you. He needs you.'

Abigail rose quickly, stung by shock and the bitter
irony of the words.

'Brett doesn't need me. He has made that all too clear.'

'But he married you.'

'Oh yes,' Abigail heard herself laugh. 'He married me. I have his name, but that is all. It was an arrangement. He needed a mother for Sophie and I. . .'

Helen Rydall studied her shrewdly. 'You are in love with him.'

'Yes.' Her hands clenched together. 'I told myself it would be enough, to be here, to be near him, to have Sophie.' She crossed to the window, unable to face the woman. 'I was a fool. I should have gone back to England, tried to forget him.' Suddenly a thought was beginning to take shape in her minds and as it grew the colour began to creep slowly back into her cheeks. 'I have to get away. I shall take the first ship back to England.'

She heard Helen's gasp of protest. 'I think you will be making a terrible mistake.'

'But surely you must see I have no choice. What is there for me here, now?'

'My dear, I think you are wrong, so very wrong. Brett loves you.'

'How can you say that? He is incapable of any feeling.'

'If you really believe that then you didn't see him as I did when he brought you home. If ever I saw a man in torment and fear of losing something he loved, it was Brett.' She went to Abigail, resting a hand on her arm. 'Are you blind, child? Why do you imagine he has gone after Peters? Is that the act of a man who doesn't care? You are his wife.'

'How can I believe it. He has always been so distant. . .cruel. He has never said. . .'

'He has been hurt once—badly. Do you imagine a

man like Brett would gladly risk that it could happen again? Does he know you love him?'

Abigail felt her nails biting into the flesh of her palms. 'It seemed the last thing he needed or desired.'

'Between you, you seem to have made a very sorry mess of it.'

'I've been a fool, a blind fool.'

'You are both fools if you allow this to happen. For pity's sake, my dear, if you love him, fight.'

'But it's too late, don't you see that? How can I possibly expect Brett to believe that my going to the Peters' place was innocent, that I didn't encourage him.' Another sickening thought came to her and she stared at the woman. 'Peters—what if he is expecting Brett? He could be waiting for him. Brett may be killed.' She was on her feet. 'I must go after him, try to stop him.'

'You would be too late and even if you weren't, how could you prevent it?'

'I must do something.'

Helen Rydall stood deliberately in front of her. 'It may be hard for you to accept,' she said, quietly, 'but perhaps it is best this way. So much was left unfinished after Elaina returned to England and then he got the news of her death. My dear, if he is ever to find peace it must be now.'

'Even if it means I may lose him?' Abigail's hands rose, shaking, to her lips.

'Is that possible? You said your marriage is nothing more than a farce, an arrangement? What have you to lose? Isn't it even possible you may find something in all this?'

Abigail buried her face in her hands, bereft of words and Helen turned, gathering up her gloves. 'I must go.'

'Oh no, I thought you would stay. Please.'

'I'm sorry, my dear, I have to get to Udaipur. I promised to be with my sister-in-law when her child is born. It's her third but she hasn't been well throughout the pregnancy so I feel I must be there.' She took Abigail's hands in her own and kissed her cheek. 'I wish you well, my dear. Brett is a fine man but stubborn, far too stubborn for his own good. He needs you. I only pray he has the good sense to realise it and doesn't let pride stand in his way.'

Abigail watched as she sat in the *dak-gharri*, her parasol raised. It was the last thing she could see, the tiny patch of yellow fading into the distance, then she returned slowly to the house wondering how she would endure the next hours of waiting. Would Brett return, and if he did would he want her to remain at Mandara?

The last of the daylight had faded and Abigail's mind, already easy prey for wild imaginings, began to fear the worst. He wouldn't be coming back. He was lying dead somewhere. But then surely she would know? Some part, deep within her, would sense it. Or was it only his anger she could feel?

Her bruised body ached but somehow she managed to slip out of her clothes and put on a robe over her thin nightgown. Exhaustion and tension were beginning to take their toll but she couldn't, daren't sleep. Not until she knew, and then she must face him, make him listen to the truth, even if there was only contempt in his eyes as he looked at her. At least then she would know.

For what seemed an eternity she paced the room, going every now and again to the window but seeing nothing. The night air was chilly and she reached for a shawl, wrapping it about her shoulders. Was it possible he had returned and somehow she hadn't heard him?

Surely he would have come to her, if only to tell her to leave Mandara. Unless he couldn't bring himself even to look at her. There was only one way to find out. Before her resolution could fail her she left her room and made her way along the gallery. She stared at his door, her hand rose, hovered, then tapped, but there was no answer. Hesitating, she half turned, then drew herself up. There was no point in running away. If he would not speak to her at least she could speak to him. With her head held high she entered the room, only to find it empty. A feeling of disappointment engulfed her. She had been so sure, the words had been ready and now they vanished, sticking in her throat like dry chaff.

For a moment she considered retracing her steps to her own room but to do so would only be to prolong the torment. She would wait there. It was hours since he had left. Surely it couldn't be much longer.

She moved slowly about the room, drawn by the maleness of it. The furnishings were luxurious but plain, devoid of the little alterations a woman would make. It was in darkness but she made no move to light the lamp as a shaft of moonlight cut a path across the floor and fell across the large bed. She moved slowly towards it and ran her fingers over the covers. After a moment she sat down letting the shawl slip from her shoulders. On impulse she lay back, resting her head against the pillows, her hand caressing the empty place next to her, and her breath caught in her throat as a wave of desire ran through her.

The sound of the door clicking gently open had her jerking upright, her heart beating so fast that she thought it would burst. He was back. In the darkness she waited, regretting now the impulse which had made her wait there. But it was too late to escape and whatever else happened she was glad, glad that he was alive. She began to rise then a voice whispered into the darkness,

'Sahib, are you there? It is I, Gita.'

Abigail froze, unable to speak as she saw the girl move slowly into the room. Her own eyes were accustomed to the darkness but the girl was not as yet aware of her own presence and Abigail heard her laugh, softly. With sickening dread she felt all her hopes wiped out. How could she even have imagined there was any chance? She felt sick. Helen had been wrong, there was nothing for which to fight. She had forgotten Gita, forgotten that other night when she had come to his room, and she had seen the girl draw his face down to kiss him passionately.

Instinctively she expelled her breath and the sound made the girl turn sharply.

'Sahib, is that you?' Abigail heard the sudden note of doubt. 'Who is it? Who is there? I shall call for the servants.'

'I wouldn't do that if I were you, Gita.' Somehow Abigail forced herself to speak and saw the girl's eyes, wide and glinting in the darkness, full of venom as they stared at her. 'You would look very foolish if you brought everyone running for no cause.'

'You. What are you doing here?'

'I think that is a question I should be asking you. You forget, I have every right to be here, I am his wife.'

The full mouth twisted convulsively. 'His wife. You say that but I know the truth. He does not love you. It is me he wants, me he turns to.'

There was something about her, about the certainty with which she flaunted her victory, that made Abigail draw herself up. Inside, her heart was pounding, but outwardly, by some miracle, she managed to maintain a mask of composure even as anger seemed to burst from her like an uncontrollable force. 'That may have been so until now, Gita, but from this moment things are going to change. You will leave this house.' She didn't know what made her say it. She was aware of nothing except some driving force from within. She may not be Brett's wife in anything but name but for the brief time she was likely to remain in his house she meant to assert her right. Trembling with every nerve in her body she faced the girl, moving closer. 'Call the servants by all means, if you wish. It will save me the trouble.'

The girl's chin rose. 'You cannot do this. He will not permit. . .'

Abigail walked calmly to the bell-pull. 'I'm afraid you are wrong. I can and will, unless you remove yourself immediately from this house and never return. You see, Gita, it is I who will not permit.'

The girl stood defiantly and Abigail felt her confidence almost desert her, but she clung to it and to the few remaining shreds of her dignity. The dark cat-like eyes were narrowed and she sensed that the girl would like to strike her and was held back only by the fear that what she had said was the truth.

'You will be sorry.' The words were hissed and Abigail flinched.

'Please leave.' Her hand held the bell-pull. In another second she must make some move or allow Gita her victory. Her face a mask of fury the girl whirled suddenly and fled.

As the door closed Abigail released a long pent-up breath and sank weakly back on to the bed, trying to still the pounding of her heart. What had she done? Suddenly the enormity of her action gripped her, yet strangely she felt no real regret. It had been an empty gesture but she had made it. It was she who would leave

Mandara never to return. At first light she would pack
her belongings. Somehow she would explain to Sophie.
It had to be done. She couldn't just walk out of the
child's life and it would be hard, saying goodbye, to
Sophie, to Mandara, to. . . Yes, it would be very hard.

She must have fallen asleep because a sudden sound
brought her back to consciousness with a start of fear. It
was still dark and it was some seconds before she realised
that she was still in Brett's room, lying on his bed. Her
hand went to her mouth, stifling the sounds of her own
breathing as she caught a slight movement in the shadows. Had Gita returned? If only she knew how long she
had been asleep. Oh what stupidity had allowed her to
remain there, to rest her head against that pillow,
dampening it with tears?

A figure moved out of the darkness, stumbled and
almost fell towards the bed. Abigail felt her lips part in a
scream which was held trapped in silence by the hand she
pressed to her mouth, willing the thudding of her heart
to quieten.

'Gita?' It was Brett's voice.

The knowledge that he had expected to find the girl
waiting for him drew a long, low gasp of pain from her as
he moved to stand beside the bed. She tried to speak, to
say something if only to let him know that it wasn't Gita,
that it was his wife, but she felt utterly incapable of
movement as she fought a wave of nausea and anger. He
paused, standing stock still for a moment as he stared
down at the figure lying on the bed. She drew back
quickly against the pillows as a shaft of moonlight cut in
through the moving cutains, but not before it had rested
briefly on his face, showing her a mask of pain-ravaged
weariness which left her sick with horror as she saw the

blood seeping from a wound in his shoulder.

She uttered an involuntary cry as she heard him stifle a groan, then he was unfastening his shirt, tugging it from the belt at his waist and flinging it from him. He swayed slightly then she heard his breath quicken as he stripped off his trousers and dropped on to the bed beside her, reaching out to draw her with angry ruthlessness towards him until her body was moulded against his and she lay trapped in the circle of his arms. They were like bands of steel, mercilessly crushing her to him and she cried out,

'No, Brett, no.'

But he didn't seem to hear and his hands began brutally to strip her of the nightdress, leaving her trembling as she felt the nakedness of her own flesh against his. She found it hard to believe this nightmare was really happening and fought him blindly, but her movements were useless against the sheer male strength of him as he plundered her mouth with his kisses, brutally arousing emotions within her which she had never known existed until then. She was shaking violently as his hands relentlessly explored her body, stroking her cheek, the line of her lips and then, when she tried to turn her head away, forcing her to him, bruising her mouth in a kiss which seemed to draw the very breath out of her.

'No, Brett, please don't,' she gasped, her head drawn back against the pillows as he released her, but it was only for an instant, then his hands moved on, becoming more insistent, more audacious in their searchings until she groaned as a sensation of pure, unbearable pleasure was dragged from her. She felt her resistance crumbling away as he tore down her defences, robbing her shred by shred of what remaining dignity she naively clung to. He was like a madman as desire drove him on—he seemed determined to possess her in spite of her struggles. Yet somehow she had to stop him, tell him that she wasn't Gita, that it was *her* body he was holding, abusing with the strength of his need to be rid of whatever demon was pursuing him. She knew that at this moment his wife, she, Abby, didn't exist. He didn't know the terrible mistake he was making.

In one swift movement he rolled over and she was pinned beneath him. Her struggles were feeble yet frenzied as his weight crushed her. It was obvious what he intended and she fought like a wild-cat, lashing out with her hands as his legs bruised her in his attempts to gain mastery. He caught her wrists effortlessly in one hand, pinioning them against the pillow. She sobbed as he buried his face against her hair and then searched again, hungrily, for her mouth. Her body arched in an attempt to deny him, and she knew instantly that it was a mistake and that there was no way she could prevent what was going to happen.

'Brett.' The scream was ripped from her. 'Don't, please. It's Abby.' For one second she felt the awful tensing of his body and hoped, prayed he would stop. She didn't want it to be like this. Even though her body ached with the senses he had aroused and went on arousing even now, as if every movement of her body seemed to drive him on, though she wanted him with every fibre of her being, it was his love she wanted, not the lust he felt for some other woman, not to be taken out of revenge for his hatred of a dead wife.

For one moment she almost thought she had won as he lay still above her, then his hands imprisoned her face and she lay rigid beneath him.

'Do you think I'm so crazed, so blind, Abby, that I don't know?'

She heard her own gasp of horror but even as she tried

to struggle she knew she was helpless.

'Don't fight me, Abby.' He moved, brutally threatening to bring down the one remaining defence she had, and she moaned with mingled pain and desire. Then as he began the slow, torturing, cruel invasion of her body, she wept as she tried to plead with him. 'I'll never forgive you. This is rape. You'll never forgive yourself.'

His fingers twisted cruelly in her hair and her eyes widened in pain as he stared down at her. 'It won't work, Abby. Don't forget I'm the man who has no conscience, no feelings. I'm going to take you, as I should have done a long time ago. After all you're my wife.' He kissed her then with a savagery which left her mouth bruised and swollen before he let her fall back against the pillows.

'Was this how it was with Peters, or was he more subtle? Did you offer yourself to him, Abby, or did you fight him the way you're fighting me? But I'm not Peters, Abby, I'm the man you married and if this is the only way I can ensure your faithfulness then this is the way it has to be, because you're mine and you'll stay mine.'

She screamed then as he moved with coldly calculated ruthlessness, and the pain seared through her body as he took her. It was like a knife thrust and yet the pain subsided and in its wake she felt a deep, throbbing ache of desire which she had never imagined existed and which she never wanted to end. Slowly, expertly, he proceeded to rob her of every shred of innocence and, wondrously, of fear. Only when his anger was finally sated and he lay breathing hard beside her, still not relinquishing his hold on her, did she finally manage to bring herself to speak.

The pain was gone. What she felt now was pity and love, a love which he would never understand.

She stared up at the ceiling, a hand flung across her eyes as she said, softly, 'It was never like that with James Peters. No matter what he told you, it wasn't true. I didn't go to him. . . give myself to him.' For a moment she thought he hadn't heard or simply refused to answer, then he raised himself and with miraculous and infinite tenderness looked down at her before taking her face in his hands and kissing her.

She trembled, awaiting the assault, but this time it didn't come. It was as if the fire had died within him and she heard the break in his voice as he said, with his head buried against hers on the pillow, 'I know. Dear God, I know, and I know I can never expect your forgiveness.'

She turned her head to stare at him incredulously. 'You . . .you know.' In the darkness she knew her face was ashen. 'But then, why?'

'Don't you see,' his voice lashed her, 'I was sick of being taunted, of having to live with what. . . she did, and the fear that it was happening all over again. I couldn't bear that. I couldn't let it happen. I needed you.'

She closed her eyes, swallowing hard. 'But I am not Elaina. I never was, never will be. I'm your wife.' Suddenly she could bear it no longer. She flung back the covers and climbed out of the bed, wincing as his assault upon her made itself felt, then, remembering her nakedness, she tried to cover her body with a sheet.

His hands stopped her and he tugged it from her and began to caress the smoothness of her back. She shivered with a mixture of pleasure and fear—fear that he would arouse her again. And she couldn't let that happen. He had needed her, wanted revenge, well he had had what he wanted, the bruises on her body proved it, but he hadn't once spoken about love and she doubted that he ever would, because Brett Farraday didn't know what it meant. Elaina had destroyed whatever human emotions he might once have had.

'Will you ever forgive me, Abby?'

She heard him without moving. She knew that if she did she would only betray herself. 'There's nothing to forgive. As you said, I'm your wife.'

For a moment she felt his hand tighten against her back, then it fell away. Seconds later she heard him dress quickly and as she turned he must have seen the question in her eyes.

'Go to sleep, Abby,' he said grimly. 'I won't trouble you again.'

She stared after him, almost afraid to interpret his words. 'But. . . you're hurt. At least let me bathe. . .'

'It's nothing. A knife wound. It looks worse than it is.'

'And. . . James Peters?'

For a moment he stood in the doorway looking at her. 'Don't worry, Abby, he won't trouble us any more. Go to sleep.'

'But where are you going? When will you be back?'

'Does it matter?' He flung the door open. I have to get out, to think. Perhaps later we can talk.'

She half rose, clutching the sheet to her. 'Brett. . . I love you.'

It was too late, he was already gone, the door had closed behind him and she was alone. He had taken her body by force when she would have given it willingly for love. But love, it seemed, was the one thing he didn't have to give.

CHAPTER
THIRTEEN

ABIGAIL woke with sunlight on her face and lay for a moment wondering where she was. As memory returned she sat up quickly. She was still in Brett's room but there was no sign of his having returned.

Pushing back the covers she slipped from the bed and returned to her own room to dress. It was little after dawn but already the air was hot and still. The storm seemed closer and suddenly she longed for it as if it could wash away the far greater storm raging in her heart.

There was no time to think or plan how her leaving was to be accomplished. It had to be now, before he could return. He had reminded her, quite ruthlessly, that she was his wife, but after what had happened she knew she couldn't stay merely so that he could exact further revenge for what Elaina had done.

The sounds of a wakening household came to her as she dressed, her mouth quivering in a fever of impatience as she dragged on a blouse and skirt, securing the belt at her waist. Her blood froze at the thought of spending the rest of her life playing a part, a wife in public whilst in private. . . She blinked away the tears. How could she stay when each time she saw him her body behaved like a traitor, when he could rouse her, make her want to respond with a kind of primitive abandonment which left him untouched. His kisses ravished her senses, mingling savagery with fire, but to him they were nothing.

A wave of tiredness swept over her but she fought it. Thrusting open the cupboards she pushed aside the gowns which had made up her trousseau. They merely added to the mockery. The only things she would take were the things she had brought with her from England. As she pushed them into the open trunk which stood beside the bed she became aware of noise and confusion in the courtyard below. At first she ignored it, kneeling to open a smaller box which had contained some of her more treasured personal items. A faint waft of lavender rose to her nostrils bringing nostalgic memories of England. Tight-lipped she folded her gowns, carelessly in her haste. One of the boys would drive her in a *dak* to the railroad. She had no idea when there would be a train but she would get to Bombay eventually, and sooner or later there would be a ship to England. Perhaps in the weeks the voyage would take she might begin to lose some of the awful numbness which seemed to have taken hold of her.

She closed the trunk, securing the heavy locks, and straightened up. Her face was pale even under the light tan she had already acquired. There was no way of knowing when Brett would return. It could be at any moment. Her glance went round the room which had become so familiar then, quickly, as if afraid of anything which might weaken her resolve, she went to the door and downstairs.

The smell of coffee brought forceful reminders that she hadn't eaten and there was no way of knowing when she would get her next meal. For that reason alone, though her stomach rebelled, she forced herself to sit and eat some of the freshly baked bread and drink the scalding coffee, wondering vaguely why Gopal was not there as usual, paying his customary attention to her needs.

She had finished her meal when he came towards her. Her mind was in turmoil, trying to assess the best means of her escape. It was possible Brett had gone straight from the Peters' place to the mine—anything to put off his return. She stared at her fob-watch. She still had to see Sophie.

'Gopal will you have one of the servants bring down the trunk from my room and arrange for someone to take me to the railroad?'

'Trunk, memsahib?'

She purposely avoided his gaze. 'Yes please, as quickly as possible.'

'But, memsahib, I am not hearing anything from the sahib that the memsahib wishes to go to the railroad.'

'No.' Her gaze implored him not to question her. 'It was rather a sudden decision. I'm afraid I have to go, Gopal. I must. Please.'

Beneath the white turban his eyes studied her with shrewd anxiety. 'It is not good, memsahib.'

'I know,' she confessed weakly. 'But to stay can do no good either, I see it now. It was foolish of me to believe otherwise. Perhaps some day he will find someone who can help him to forget, but that someone is not me.' She looked directly at him. 'Which is why you must help me. I want to go now, quietly, before he returns. It is best.'

To her dismay, however, she saw that he was shaking his head. 'But it is not possible, memsahib, even if I wished. You cannot leave now.'

Panic rose. 'But I must, surely you don't mean to prevent me?'

'I would not, if it is what the memsahib desires, but it is not safe.'

'I don't understand. I've ridden out before. If necessary I will take a *syce* to escort me. If there is no *dak* I will take a horse.'

'The memsahib does not understand. It is because of
Jhuma.' He saw the bewilderment in her eyes. 'Tiger, a
man-eater, memsahib. He has been seen and he has
already tasted blood.'

A spasm of fear tightened her stomach. 'You mean he
is in this area?'

'He runs ahead of the beaters, but do not be afraid,
the gates have been closed and the men are armed.'

Stunned she looked at him, realising now what had
been the cause of the commotion she had heard earlier.
Then her eyes widened with horror. 'But my husband is
out there. He is in danger. We must do something.' She
didn't know what she intended but suddenly the bearer's
hand was on her arm, restraining her.

'There is nothing the memsahib can do.'

'We must try to warn him.'

'It would be no use. But have no fear, the sahib knows
Jhuma. They are old adversaries. The sahib has hunted
him many times.'

'And failed to find him.' A shudder convulsed her
body. He might be lying out there alone, injured or
worse. She thought of the trunks packed and waiting and
knew that she couldn't leave now, not until she knew he
was safe. Afterwards. . . pray God there would be an
afterwards.

'You say Jhuma has been seen? Where?'

'In a village, memsahib, a few miles to the east. He
killed a child.'

She pressed a hand to her stomach feeling the nausea
rise. 'But how do you know he will come this way or that
he will kill again so soon?'

'A cat who has tasted blood must always have more.
The scent of it drives him to madness until in the end he
will lose his cunning in his desire to satisfy that thirst.

Traps are being set, memsahib. Live goats are being tethered out in the open to lure him.'

'And if he doesn't take them?'

'The he is looking for a bigger kill and only a bullet will stop him.'

A film of sweat bathed her skin yet she felt cold. 'Put someone to watch for my husband's return. The gates must be opened the moment he is in sight, is that clear?' She stayed him as he turned away. 'Wait, is he armed?'

The Indian's eyes narrowed. 'No, memsahib, it is his rule always to take the gun but this time. . .'

'Dear God, he won't stand a chance.'

'The sahib is not a man to take risks, memsahib. This country is in his blood. He knows its dangers. He may even see the villagers as they drive Jhuma ahead of them and if it is so, he will be safe.'

'Yes, of course you're right.' Reason told her it was true but it didn't lessen her fears. She left Gopal and hurried to Sophie's room. The entire household seemed uneasy, as if it had a kind of premonition, a sense of impending doom. Her eyes caught sight of figures crouched on the high walls their eyes scanning the arid landscape. Surely nothing could get into Mandara unseen?

Reaching Sophie's room she paused outside the door, giving herself time to appear calm, but as she entered, a smile on her lips, it faded instantly as she saw only the old *ayah* who was gathering up items of discarded clothing. The woman salaamed, smiling her cracked-tooth smile, and Abigail felt a shaft of ice-cold fear run through her.

'Where is Sophie, where is the child?'

The woman spoke in her own native tongue.

'I don't understand.' Abigail went to her, quickly, pleading, 'What are you trying to say, where is she?' Her hands encompassed the emptiness of the room in an attempt to convey her meaning. The *ayah* spoke again and this time she caught the word *'syce'*. Colour drained from her face. 'You mean she has gone riding. Oh, dear God. Jhuma.'

The *ayah's* leathery hand stayed her, the dark eyes suddenly full of fear which became contagious. 'Jhuma.' She repeated the word, uttering a loud wail which rose hysterically until Abigail shook her.

'Listen to me, listen. Where? Tell me which way she has gone.' Mercilessly she dragged the woman to the window. 'Which way? Show me.'

It was no good, the woman either didn't understand or was too hysterical to respond. Close to panic Abigail left her and ran, stumbling over her skirts, to find Gopal. She was almost sobbing as she reached him, vaguely aware that he supported her.

'Sophie is out there, do you understand? She has gone riding. We must go after her.' Her heartbeats were suffocating her. It was more than she could bear to lose Brett and Sophie. 'Open the gates, tell them to open the gates.' She clasped a hand to her eyes. 'Oh Brett, where are you?'

Dimly she was aware of Gopal calling out commands. He put her gently aside, his face tight-lipped, then his head rose sharply and he seemed to be listening.

'What are you doing?' she cried. 'Sophie is out there. Make them open the gates.'

'Listen, memsahib.' His hand entreated her silence but it was hard to hear anything above the pounding of her heart. Then it came, at first so faintly, so distant, that she could almost believe she had imagined it. Then it

came again, gradually louder and louder. Her fists clenched. 'Drums?'

'They have sighted Jhuma and are driving him before
them with the noise.'

She thought she would faint. She swayed, then fought
against Gopal's restraining hand. 'Let me go. That
animal is out there and they are driving him straight to
Sophie.'

'Go back, memsahib. I will find the little one.'

Before she could answer he was running, shouting to
the men at the gate, and only then did she realise that he
meant to go alone. The sound of the drums was coming
closer and closer and now she could hear the shouts of
the villagers, as ruthlessly and monotonously they pur-
sued the killer.

The gates were swung back and in the same instant she
had a blurred image of a horse and rider and a figure,
dark legs and bare feet running. Sophie was clinging to
the neck of her pony, the reins lost, her face ashen white.
She screamed and Abigail ran to her, snatching the child
from the saddle, pushing aside the sweat-bathed hair.

'Thank God, I was so afraid.'

'The *syce* heard the drums and said we must get back.
What is it?'

Gopal was beside them, taking the child from her.
'The danger is not yet over, memsahib. It is best you go
into the house. The sahib would flay me alive were
anything to befall the memsahib and little one. Please,'
he implored, 'go back.'

She stared wildly at him. 'But my husband is still out
there.'

'You can do nothing. By now he will have heard the
drums and will be returning. Believe me, it is so.'

He was trying to reassure her but she wasn't deceived.

Without any means to defend himself Brett would be completely helpless.

'I'm frightened.' Sophie whimpered.

Her hand caressed the child's soft curls. 'Yes, I know, darling, but look, the men are keeping watch and they have guns. We won't come to any harm, isn't that so, Gopal?'

He smiled. 'Indeed, the little one need not be afraid. Jhuma is old and has lost his cunning, otherwise he would not have allowed himself to be seen. You will see, his days are numbered.'

Abigail's mouth quivered. 'There, you see?' She swept the Indian a look of gratitude as he carried Sophie back to the house and up to her room. She forced herself to chatter as they went but her mouth was dry, the noise of the beaters set her nerves on edge as they came closer and ever closer. If Brett had heard them why was he not here?

Her movements were mechanical as she stripped off Sophie's dress and helped her to change. The small pale face kept returning anxiously to the window.

Making the action seem casual, Abby went over and closed the shutters, drawing the curtains. 'Why don't you lie down for a while. Close your eyes—or would you like some lemonade first?'

'Yes please.'

'Right then you shall have some. I'll fetch it.' She bent to kiss the pale cheek before making her way to her own room. A glass and jug stood on a tray. Her hands shook as she poured the cool, refreshing liquid then tightened as her gaze fell on the trunk. It seemed an eternity since she had flung her things into it. It had all seemed so easy, so straightforward, but now nothing was certain any more, except that she wanted to see Brett, to hear his voice. He had to be safe, that was all that mattered.

One of the curtains fluttered, bringing her from her reverie. For some reason her heart missed a beat as she stood, transfixed, until she realised it had been nothing more than the stirring of a breeze. An uneasy laugh rasped in her throat. She was letting her imagination run away with her. No animal, however wild or cunning, could escape the relentless pursuit of those drums and the guns positioned in readiness. It had no choice but to run, unless it could find a hiding place, and there was nowhere. . .

Slowly, very slowly her hand crept to her throat, then she was flinging the door open and running. 'Sophie!' She stumbled blindly to the door just as it opened and Sophie came towards her.

'I can't sleep. Why have the drums stopped?'

Had they stopped? She hadn't been aware of it until now but Sophie was right. For some reason the silence was even more terrifying. There was a deathly unnatural quiet as if everyone and everything waited, holding its breath.

Her voice was little more than a whisper. 'I don't know, darling.' Standing at the head of the stairs she looked down into the hall below. It was deserted. Where were the servants? Where was Gopal? Calling his name she began to move with Sophie. They were perhaps half-way down the stairs when she heard the soft thud and saw a shadow move across the hall—except that it was no shadow.

She felt Sophie stiffen beside her, heard the gasping intake of the child's breath. Her own blood seemed to be frozen in her veins. 'Don't move.'

The tiger was in the house. Somehow, in spite of its relentless pursuers, it had managed to invade the walls in desperate search for sanctuary. She saw the power of it

in the rippling movements of its shoulders as it padded
softly across the tiled floor. Then it reached the foot of
the stairs and for one horrifying instant their stricken
gazes met.

Sophie screamed. Unthinking, Abigail swept her into
her arms and tried to run. It was useless, even as she
compelled her feet to move she knew it. Sobbing, she fell
as her skirts tangled about her ankles and she threw
herself over Sophie, waiting, knowing that at any second
she would feel the animal's hot breath and the merciless
teeth tear at her flesh. Her breath seemed to burn in her
lungs and she was sobbing wildly, but it didn't come.

The door crashed open. Daring to raise her head she
saw Gopal in the same instant that the great cat swung
about, diverted by the sound. She saw Gopal's eyes, white
in the darkness of his face as he recognised their danger.

'Do not move, memsahib.'

The cat snarled and leapt. Abigail heard herself
scream. She saw the gun in the Indian's hands and heard
the shot, but the animal had scented its prey. It leapt and
struck. The rifle cut an arc into the air and fell, spinning
across the floor. She heard Gopal's strangled cry and the
tiger was on him. The rest was a nightmare as the flailing
figure threshed beneath the savage onslaught.

Fighting the waves of nausea and terror Abigail
moved, not even knowing what she did. Her hands
thrust Sophie away, then without even looking to see if
the child had obeyed she moved towards the fallen rifle.
Tears blinded her. Where was it? Had it spun further
than she realised? There was blood. Faintness swept like
a black wave over her. Somehow she fought it off then
her fingers touched cold metal. She dragged the rifle to
her, her fingers clumsy with fear. She had seen Brett fire
one once, but how? Panic took hold. She swung the

barrel towards the animal, its bulk concealing the now still man beneath, and fired. The sound combined with her scream and she fell, sobbing, rocked by the force of the blast.

Vaguely she saw the creature slump and knew that someone was coming towards her, calling her name.

Opening her eyes she had a miraculous vision of Brett's face, grim and white as he stared down at her. She clung to him and he went to his knees, holding her.

'Abby, dear God, are you hurt?'

'Brett, I was so afraid.'

His hands smoothed the hair from her eyes, tilting her face backwards as he bent to kiss her. She could feel the beating of his heart through his shirt.

'I thought I'd never see you again. I thought you were dead.' Then she remembered. 'Gopal. Brett, he saved our lives.' Dimly she was aware that Sophie had run to her *ayah* who was weeping. Abby turned, half rising to go to Gopal. Brett tried to prevent her but it was too late. The Indian lay still, his body covered in blood, as the animal was dragged away. She shrank back, burying her head against Brett's chest.

'He's badly hurt. There's nothing we can do for him.' He spoke softly and his arms tightened about her, then his hand raised her face and his mouth came down on hers, tasting the salt of tears before he swept her up and carried her up the stairs and into his room. He lay her on the bed and stood looking down at her, something in his expression making her tremble. The anguish had gone from his eyes to be replaced by steel-cold anger. She tried to sit up but he pushed her back and once again she was aware of his strength and her own vulnerability as he leaned over her.

'Don't ever ask me to let you go again.' His voice

rasped, savagely. 'I can't do it, do you understand?' He
was shaking her so that her teeth rattled. 'I almost let
you persuade me. God knows I hate myself for what I
did to you last night, but I'd do it again, I'd do anything
to keep you. Do you know what I'm saying?'

Breathlessly she stared up at him. His fingers touched
her face, traced the marks of the bruises. 'I love you,
Abby, I need you, do you understand that. I won't let
you go. When I heard you scream I thought it was you
and my blood ran cold. I couldn't bear it if I were to lose
you. I won't let you go.'

She trembled as she stared up at him. She knew without a doubt that he was capable of doing what he threat-
ened and yet, strangely, that was not what troubled her.

'Elaina,' she murmured and saw the grim hard line of
his mouth as he lowered himself down beside her.

'Elaina is dead and I've been a fool, a crazy, demented
fool.' His hand touched the curve of her cheek. 'Did I
hurt you very much?'

She raised a trembling hand to his lips, silencing the
words. 'Can you also forget Gita?'

'Gita?' He frowned. 'There is nothing to forget.'

'But I saw her. She came to your room. I saw her kiss
you.' She couldn't meet his gaze, but his hands drew her
towards him.

'What did you see?'

Her voice seemed to be trapped in her throat. 'You
kissed her.'

'Are you sure that's what you saw, Abby? Are you
sure it wasn't this?' And taking her hands he lifted them,
lowering his face down to hers. 'Isn't that what happened? You saw Gita kiss me.'

Her answer was lost as his kiss became reality. She
closed her eyes, revelling in the ecstasy of emotions

which now sprang to life like a fire consuming everything in its path, then she broke away. 'But you thought it was Gita in your bed. I heard you say her name.'

'Because she had tried before to make something of our relationship.' He held her gaze. 'I admit she was beautiful, she was there, and there was a time when I needed. . . not Gita, but someone, anyone, just to try and rid myself of this terrible anger. But I never loved her, or any woman, I realise that now, until you came to Mandara.'

Her voice seemed to have deserted her. His presence as he bent over her was like a threat, yet one she didn't want to avoid. Her hands reached up and she drew him close and his mouth took hers, possessively, but this time without the brutality she had known only a few hours before. He released her at last.

'I asked last night for your forgiveness. . .'

'And I said there was nothing to forgive.'

He stared at her incredulously. 'In spite of what I did? If you had any idea of how I hate myself. . .'

'I don't believe you knew what you were doing. I think in your heart you believed I had betrayed you, just as Elaina did. Oh yes,' she saw the look in his eyes. 'I know what happened now. I only wish you could have told me the truth yourself. It would have explained so many things.'

He gripped her arms, his face tense. 'But would you have stayed? I had to be sure. I wanted you here and I was prepared to do anything. . . anything to make you stay.'

She watched as he got to his feet. 'You wanted me here for Sophie's sake in the beginning.'

'No.' His voice was edged with doubt. 'That's not true. Oh it may have been, partly. Sophie was my excuse.

I wanted her and you, both of you.' He looked at her. 'I warn you, Abby, I don't care how I have to fight . . .'

She got up and went to him, slowly. 'You don't need to fight any more. I'll stay. As your wife.' She caught the brief look of disbelief in his eyes then she was in his arms, kissing him, her fingers touching the ravages on his face. 'You have me and you have Sophie.' Gently, as some memory stirred, she released herself from him and went to the desk from which she drew a box. Taking something from it she returned to him and held out the ring. 'Lady Flixton gave me this. She asked me to keep it and return it one day to Sophie. Perhaps you should give it to her.'

He stared at the ruby glinting in the palm of his hand. 'I'd forgotten how beautiful it was,' he murmured and she saw the glimmer of anger in his eyes. 'Yet Elaina always hated it.' His hand closed over it. 'I don't think this is for Sophie, nor is it for you. I have something else. Wait, don't move.'

She stood as he left the room, wondering idly what he meant. He returned and without a word stood behind her, fastening the clasp of a gold chain round her neck. 'This is for you, this *is* you, my love.'

She felt the breath tighten in her throat as he led her to a mirror then she gasped as she saw the pale, beautiful brilliance of the stones at her throat.

'Sapphires for you, my dearest, beloved wife, because there is a gentleness in you, a quiet depth like a pool which hides nothing, not even its fear. But I promise, you need never fear me again.'

She turned slowly in his arms. 'And I love you too, my dearest, dearest Brett.'

His mouth came down over hers then he swept her up in his arms and carried her to the bed. But this time she knew she need not be afraid, nor ever again.